C

The K

By Celia Loren

* * *

Also From Celia Loren:

The Vegas Titans Series

Devil's Kiss (Widowmakers Motorcycle

Club) by Celia Loren

Crushing Beauty (Harbingers of Sorrow

MC) by Celia Loren

CRUSH

The Kelly Brothers

* * *

By Celia Loren

CONTENTS

Prologue

* * *

San Diego, 2005.

I remember exactly what I was wearing the day I fell in love for the first time. I remember too the color of the sky (bad-air-quality avocado), the newspaper headlines ("Forest Fires Near Big Sur"), and the music on the bus radio (Sheryl Crow). But most of all, I remember the boy. He was already five foot six, which was tall for a ten year old, and he was rocking blonde tips and that gelled flip that was so popular for two months in the nineties—in other words, he was already perfect.

There were fifteen of us in Mr. Seidman's P.E. class, and though it must have been well before noon, we were already sweating on the soccer field. It was the last day of my first week at George Washington Carver Elementary School, and as of that humid Friday, I'd yet to make a single friend.

"We're doing four laps around the field today, folks. That'll make a mile," Mr. Seidman said.

I remember the gym teacher, too—he had the fussy, inflated look of a snowy owl and was about as friendly.

"Now, the middle-schoolers run a mile," Seidman hooted. "So each and every one of you who completes this task will be ahead of the curve."

At this news, the class had broken up into little tittering groups, much to my lonely-girl dismay. My Dad had told me that all I needed to do to adapt to our new city was "smile and be myself!" but the social hierarchy at Carver was apparently having none of my Midwestern charms. There was, on one end of the spectrum, Melora Handy and her band of prissy followers. They called themselves The Ponytails. On the other side were Corinne Laughlin-Moe and Katie Delft. They liked to bring caterpillars to class and let them crawl all over their arms during lessons—and even they, it seemed, didn't want to kick it with the new kid. This made me—the motherless, gung-ho, corn-fed, Nebraska transplant—a persona non grata. A total pariah. A freak.

"And lookie what we have here!" Mr. Seidman cried, shading his eyes and directing our attention toward the gym doors. You could hear the excitement in his voice—it was clear that some Golden God was about to descend into our midst. And just like something out of Greek mythology, the object of our class' attention started to sprint towards us, running faster than anyone I'd ever seen up close.

"Who is that?" I asked Corinne, breathless. She was pretty preoccupied with her caterpillars but still managed to spare the sprinter a withering glance.

"That's Chase Kelly. He's been out sick all week."

I actually repeated the name to myself, loving how the K sounds rolled across my tongue. Chase. Kelly. He seemed to be smiling at us, as his little blonde head bobbed across the pitch. I saw two neat rows of braces on his teeth, glinting in the sunlight. Every girl paused, conversations halted—just while we watched the kid run. Chase Kelly had the easy, thoughtless, watchable stride of a cheetah. Moving quickly came natural to him.

Chase was more gangly than muscular back then, but it was immediately clear from Mr. Seidman's greeting that this sexy animal was the favored athlete of the whole fifth grade.

"Mr. Kelly!" our teacher cried, thumping Chase on the back as he landed, un-winded, amongst us. "Glad to see your flu has flown the coop. Boys and girls, Mr. Kelly here can run a five-minute mile. So you should all be aiming for his dust when we do our warm-up."

Chase smiled a little bashfully, then puffed up his chest. He'd worn a Spongebob Squarepants shirt, and that only seemed like more evidence of his star quality—he had good taste in cartoons. This was the first time a boy made my heart beat faster, my palms grow sweaty, my mouth go dry. The Meloras and the Katies around me all seemed to fade away while Chase stood there, sizing up his competition. That is, until Mr. Seidman blew the whistle.

"GO!" my gym teacher bellowed to the sky. We started scampering, and I zeroed in fast on my mission. My purpose at Carver had suddenly taken shape. I needed to run with Chase Kelly. Past him, if possible. I needed that boy to see my hair streaming behind me in his peripherals, so he could see that I, too, was worth knowing.

And so I ran. I passed The Ponytails, who were never dressed for gym anyways—preferring to wear constricting mini-skirts that were just this side of the Carver dress code. Katie and Corinne could eat my dust. It was easy, once I gave myself up to the fact: I simply had to reach Chase, or die trying. I ran that day like I'd never run before, and have never replicated since. After the first lap and a half, I was within spitting distance. By the second, sweat was pouring off my back and down my Blink-182 tank top, but our classmates were falling behind.

"Not bad for a girl!" he yelled, pausing briefly to glance over his shoulder. "Where'd you learn to run?" I was concentrating so hard on the finish line, it took a moment to register that Chase Kelly was actually speaking to me. Were I not otherwise occupied, I swear I could have fainted.

"My—mom," I wheezed. Talking was hard. "Where'd you? Learn to run?"

We rounded the goal-posts a third time, and for a moment, I burst ahead of him. Glancing back, I saw that the two of us had an easy lead over our classmates, and the people closest to us were still about a third of a lap behind. So, I slowed down. Until we were neck and neck.

"My Dad taught me," Chase gasped finally, after he too had determined our lead was sufficient. "Right before my parents got divorced." When I looked over, I saw that Chase had a wryness in his eye. His expression, even constricted with effort, suggested an intelligence surpassing that of the average fifth grader. He was being ironic. I concluded, from this one face, that Chase was funny and wise.

"My parents are divorced, too." I yelled. The air ripped from my lungs. I didn't dare to speak again, lest the stitch that was already growing in my side bring me to my knees. I was content to run side by side with Chase Kelly, in companionable silence. I was almost sorry when we reached the finish line.

"Way to go, Ms. Lynne!" Mr. Seidman yelled. And after a long pause in which I struggled to catch my breath, my classmates trickled in behind us. Melora raised her eyebrows at me with something resembling approval. For the first time all week, the fifth grade seemed to notice me. I looked up to smile at Chase Kelly, imagining that our friendship had been sealed on the track—but he wasn't beside me anymore. For a second, I panicked. It still seemed possible that I could have dreamed him. So I squinted along the hazy horizon, past the basketball court, the tetherball poles, the rusty old playground—all while Mr. Seidman rattled off everyone's mile time.

I found Chase again by the big red slide, the one where the Ponytails liked to gather and talk accessories. He was sitting on the wood-chips, head bent low in conversation with someone. He didn't look sweaty or winded at all. I didn't recognize his companion from the back, though there was something about the other boy's honey-blonde hair that seemed familiar. It was only when I came up close behind them that it occurred to me to be shy.

"Hey," I ventured, eyes locked on Chase. "That was fun, back there. I never got to tell you—I'm Avery Lynne."

After I spoke, there was a horrible pause in which it seemed like everything could collapse. Chase squinted up at me like he was struggling to remember who I was. But just then, his buddy turned around, and I saw that he was squinting up at me, too. I couldn't help but laugh. They had the exact same expression, the exact same face.

"Oh my God!" I giggled. "You're–"

"This butthead is my brother, Brendan," Chase said, flicking a wood-chip in the direction of his doppelganger. The other Kelly boy was a near-mirror image of his brother, except for a few key details. Brendan wore a single silver ring in his ear. Brendan had skater-boy hair, which fell in soft waves around his shoulders. Brendan didn't wear braces, but he was rocking an oversized t-shirt for the Red Hot Chili Peppers—easily my second-favorite band, after Blink.

"Avery's parents are divorced, too," Chase said to his brother. Then he smiled at me, and I knew I was safe in at least one Kelly's estimate. Still, I waited for Brendan to say something comforting, or smile at me, too. Something about the kid intimidated me from the get-go.

After a long pause, Brendan Kelly peeled himself off the wood-chips. Though it didn't seem in line with anything I knew about identical twins, I was shocked to see that the other Kelly boy stood about an inch taller than his brother. He seemed runtier, despite this. Somehow more drawn and bookish than his brother.

"So you guys had the flu?" I said, for something to say.

Brendan just kept staring at me, until Chase started to chuckle with discomfort. But I was emboldened by my mile time, and let him stare me down. I figured I had nothing to hide, and everything to gain.

"Did you know," Brendan said at last, with an eerie gravity: "That if your hand is bigger than your face, you're an idiot?"

I was so eager to please the Kelly twins, I fell for that dumb line. After I opened my palm in front of my face, Brendan Kelly hit me lightly—but square—on the nose bone, and all three of us dissolved into improbable giggles.

I fell for the twins that day, and the day after, and the month after, and the years after. All this time, I've been falling.

Chapter One

* * *

Savannah, Georgia 2014

"Name one great artist who ever quit at something."

"Umm, John Lennon."

"Okay, that's one."

"Probably Kafka, right? De Kooning. Virginia Woolf..."

"That's not what I meant."

"Sylvia Plath..."

"Ugh! Fine!" From her perch on the bed, Zooey hurls a ball of rainbow-patterned socks in my direction. "You win. But don't think for one second that abandoning your dearest friend at art school makes you Virginia Woolf."

My friend and I exchange a sad smile, as has become our habit this week. I kind of waited until the last minute to tell Zo that I wouldn't be coming back to Savannah in the fall, so I can't exactly blame her for giving me crap. Especially since she's my one true blue these days.

I came to art school last August so convinced that I'd become part of a whole new crew of thoughtful, nerdy weirdoes just like me—only to find that a lot of the same popularity hierarchies I'd hated in high school were still par for the pre-adult course. After I'd found Zooey during Welcome Week (and after we'd bonded over a shared disdain for certain abstract expressionists), we'd become pretty much inseparable. And if the tables were turned—if it were her leaving me stranded at school without so much as an explanation—I'd be pissed as hell.

"I just wish you'd tell me why," my friend says, for the umpteenth time. "Or at least, tell me if it's something I did."

"It's nothing you did. I swear."

This much is true. The person who 'did' it is still in the picture, though, and I can't bear to spend three more years avoiding his smirks. I can't bear to be trapped in classes next to him, where I'd have to hear him wax poetic about sculpture and other bullshit and being applauded for his "insight." It was hard enough going to the counselor the morning after and being asked all those horrible questions. And later, at the disciplinary hearing—watching him lie to my face. The memories could still make bile rise in my throat.

The city no longer felt safe to me, and no part of my art school dream remained intact—so yes, I was heading back to Western skies. And no, I wasn't able to tell my friend why I was such a profound failure of a reinvention. To be honest, I was worried that Zooey's opinion of me would change. Not in a way that she'd mean for it to— Zooey was the most understanding person I'd ever met— but something in her manner was bound to shift if she learned the truth about my leaving. She'd start to pity me. She'd want to crusade against my enemies, to adopt all of my fears like they were her own. And I was in such a wretched place, it just didn't seem fair to bring someone else down to my level. I knew it was stupid—but the 'it,' the 'him,' the horror that had happened—had left me feeling soiled.

"I think I hear your Dad's car," Zooey stands, and goes to the window. "Yup. There's old Frank."

"The pumpkin, come to take me away."

"You promise you'll Skype? And visit, maybe?"

"I'll Skype."

Zooey watches my father as he putters toward the dorm's entrance. He doesn't know the full truth, either. But Frank and I have the kind of relationship where he doesn't ask many questions. Ours is a silent alliance, grounded in guilt and mutual respect.

"You're sure things won't just be worse for you? At a big old state school like that?" Something in Zo's tone makes me glance up from my seat on the suitcase. I should give her credit. Zooey might have picked up on more about my sudden departure than I realized. She could be offering me one more chance to explain myself.

"I really want to be near my Dad, Zo. It's not like he's doing all that well, by himself in that big house."

"But he's a grown-up. You're just a teenage dirtbag."

"For one more month." Zooey doesn't look convinced. "And besides. I do have some high-school friends who stayed home and went to state. This girl Melora–"

"The Ponytail chick? I thought you hated her."

I actually only hate one person, but our goodbye didn't feel like the right moment to be splitting hairs. In lieu of a confession, I just smile sadly again.

"Okay, okay. I'm not trying to deprive you of friends because I'm jealous or anything," Zooey concedes, her voice cheeky as all hell. "I just worry."

"Well, don't worry so much."

"It's just such a bummer! I meet one cool person at college, and she's skipping town on me."

"There are loads of cool people in your college future, I'm sure of it. Now come give me a super-emotional hug before Frank storms in."

We're already too late: I can hear my Dad's strained breathing before I see his shadow, falling wide across the sick-colored linoleum. Frank's a big guy. He used to be head of security for San Diego University, before he retired. These days, he intimidates crossword puzzles.

"Wait, I remember! Those twin guys! Won't they be at school with you?" I hold tighter to Zooey's back, so I can avoid showing her my reddening face. The Kellys. Okay, sure, they've crossed my mind. The fact that I mentioned those bums to anyone at college suddenly strikes me as...childish. I hope my Dad isn't listening.

"I haven't been close with those two in forever," I say, hoping my words come across as casual. I don't know why I feel like I'm lying—for this part, at least, is the truth.

"I remember those little blondies!" calls Frank, who takes the moment to step fully into our room and sit down heavily on my roommate's bead. I break away from Zooey and turn to my Dad, who grins at us like it's any other day. Like he didn't just drive a thousand miles to fetch his failed daughter from Georgia. "Mac and Jason, right? You three couldn't be separated."

"Brendan and Chase, Dad. And we could be separated, actually. The three of us didn't hang out much past the beginning of high school," I don't embellish this story, and both Zo and Frank seem content to let the facts lie. I guess it isn't really a headline, anyways. People drift apart from their middle-school friends. That's kind of SOP, in fact.

But I can't deny to myself that I've been thinking about the Kelly boys. Those mop-tops even appeared to me in a dream the other night, for the first time in years. I was back on the track team, doing wind-sprints with Chase while Brendan yelled ridiculous things at us from the bleachers. The three of us went out for pizza afterwards, like always. But instead of racing our bikes home, to the respective nests where our single parents toiled away in the shadows of deep depressions the dream ended with me standing on the table at Fioro's, rotating around so they could see from all angles. I can't remember anything much after that, just that the two of them clapped and clapped for me.

* * *

Dad tunes the car radio to NPR as we leave Savannah behind. In my head, I whisper little goodbyes to all the old buildings in and around Chatham County. The low-hanging Spanish moss, obscuring every doorway. Those lush, humid, swampy greens, and the battered white exteriors of old houses. This really has been a beautiful place to study art. I feel the bile begin to rise up in my throat again. I'm sad to be leaving, yes, but more than that—I'm angry. One part of me feels like a failure for letting one night with one cretin ruin this amazing place for me. But another part, the part that's turning in on itself, is happy to see all this Southern Gothic shit go, hopefully along with the memories it brings. I wonder if I'll ever come back here again.

My Dad clears his throat beside me—an ancient sign, in our language, that he's ready to listen if I'm willing to talk. But I don't take the bait.

"So I spoke to Mrs. Woyzeck in the admissions department," Dad says, after we've cleared city limits. "And I think we're a go! You can start as a second-year in August, provided you take a couple make-up cores this semester. English and such. How does that sound?"

Super, I don't say. More English and Science. Exactly what I was trying to avoid with the whole "art school" thing. Instead, I reach across the seat and pat my Dad lightly on the shoulder. We aren't a particularly physical family—we don't really hug or kiss on the cheek or anything like that—but I can recognize that it must have been a small pain for him to bug his former colleagues at SDU into admitting his deadbeat daughter on a last-minute transfer. Not that I haven't done well in Savannah, but it's a tall order to make credits like "Textiles" and "Eighteenth Century Brush Technique" transfer to a big state school.

"What do you think you're gonna major in?"

"I don't know, Dad."

"Not...art?"

"I dunno. Maybe it's time for a change." I lean my head against the window, directing my gaze towards my phone. Zooey's already pinged me with a dozen sad-faced SnapChats and texts. I hope I'm not making the biggest mistake of my life.

"It's funny you should have mentioned those Kelly boys," my Dad says, after another mile or so has passed us by. In spite of the rain cloud I'm under, I feel myself perking up. "They're both at SDU, you know. And I read something in the paper the other day about the littler one—"

"They're twins, Dad!"

"The physically littler one. Don't be a wiseass."

"Brendan?"

"The one who'd always eat our fruit roll-ups, and blame it on his brother. Real quick with a dirty joke. That's Brendan?"

I smile.

There was definitely no one in Savannah quite like the Kellys—and maybe that's why their memories have been surfacing so much. I lost touch with my two middle-school best friends when the pressures of prom and Homecoming took over, but if I'm being honest, I never stopped keeping an eye on the twins. The treehouse fort we all built behind the creek in my backyard might have toppled over time, but there remains something about those two. Maybe some people just stick with you, in spite of reason and time. Some people stick, and direct traffic in your autobiography, and won't be shaken away no matter how many years pass by.

"He went a little off the rails in high-school, right? Didn't that Brendan kid—he pulled a quick stint in Juvie, right?"

"He was arrested but never charged. Resisting arrest and disturbing the peace." God, I remember that night. Too funny.

"Sounds like a winner. Well, anyways. Mrs. Woyzeck says he's calmed down, some. He came to mind because his rock n' roll band has been getting on the radio a little. When we get a bit closer in, I'll see if we can pick them up."

"Local radio?"

"California. So, I guess?" Dad flashes me a quick smile, and it feels as quick and forbidden as a burp. "Not really my cup of tea, but I thought you'd be interested to know that there are still some arty types in our neck of the woods."

Well, good for Brendan Kelly. What little I knew of his "band" could be summarized in few words: basement, weed, free-form-jazz-odyssey. There was a short time toward the beginning of high school when I still hung out with the Kellys; Melora hadn't fully sunk her claws into Chase yet, and Brendan hadn't fallen in with his whole Lords of Dogtown crew. I remember plenty of eighth-grade evenings spent baked in the smelly enclave that was the "littler" Kelly brother's basement studio, passing around a bowl and listening to Bob Dylan and the Grateful Dead on vinyl. If memory served, Brendan's band wasn't any good, but the way his honey-blonde hair fell into his eyes while he played the bass guitar had been useful motivation for a kinda-sorta-groupie.

When I catch his eye in the rearview mirror, Dad is smiling at me again.

"And you're sure you never went out with one of those two?"

"Da-ad!"

"Two boys were knocking around the house day and night for years, and not one of 'em ever once took you to a dance?"

"Dad, men and women can be just friends sometimes. Like you and Mrs. Woyzeck." Frank raises his eyebrows like he's about to burst my bubble, but mercifully falls silent again.

"Whatever you say, Avery," he says, not bothering to conceal his smile now. "Whatever you say." I close my eyes. I let Savannah drift away, and live for a while in my dreams.

Chapter Two

* * *

During the last three weeks I've spent in my childhood home, lurking in one of two rooms and watching a shit-ton of reality TV, Dad and I didn't bother to take my bags out of the trunk—so it's easy to unpack when I get to my new dorm. What's less easy to unpack is the student body of SDU: unlike in Savannah, where three-plus piercings and a neon-dye job was the norm, this California state school is a sea of jocks, Valley Girls, and casual hippies.

"Don't be so judgmental," my Dad murmurs at me, somewhat clairvoyantly. He's got a spring in his step, which makes one of us. Security guards keep doffing their caps to him, like he's a war buddy. Who knew the secret campus security alliance ran so deep?

A gangly hippie kid drifts by in a baja. He takes one look at my Dad's beat-up old Gremlin and nods his approval.

Avery, I don't think we're in the South anymore.

"Fuck me—are you the new girl?" The voice behind this remark is shrill and nasal, kind of like what's-her-face on Will & Grace. The tiny little person attached to the sound is all of five foot two, and her dark brown hair is pulled back into a taut...ponytail.

"Oh-my-god, I'm Tara Rubenstein. You're new here?" Tara Rubenstein pushes an invisible strand of hair behind her ear. She appears the epitome of perky: her face is spotted with light brown freckles, her teeth are glittery white with veneers. She's wearing yoga pants. Zooey and I used to have an awful habit of making fun of girls in yoga pants, back in Savannah. We called it "Camel Toe Watch."

My Dad taps at the back of my knee with the toe of his boot. I concede: the old man has a point. I need to make friends at my new school. I have to embrace the change I orchestrated in the first place.

"Hey, Tara," I grumble. "Yeah. I'm headed up to the third floor."

"302?"

"Yeah, 302."

"I know everything about the third floor," Tara puffs out her meager chest. "Because I'm fucking the RA." I laugh, surprised, but my new roommate just flashes her veneers. I can practically feel my Dad's whole body frowning, behind us. He's not a fan of swearing, or, I imagine, sexually empowered twenty year old girls. "You ever need any of those extra condoms they leave out in bowls everywhere, or special discount packages to, like, the roller rink? You talk to me."

I laugh easily, waiting for Tara to join me in a roommate-bonding kinda way—but she just smiles tightly again, dropping some of the perky facade in the process. It's actually a little...maniacal. I can't tell if she's kidding.

"I like your hair," Tara says quickly. "You guys need help moving stuff? I'm little, but I'm strong."

Without waiting for a response, my new roomie heads to the Gremlin's trunk and hoists my paint-box out, resting it high on her shoulder.

"Wait—actually, you can leave that one," I mutter. Tara cocks her head at me, like a bird—and for a second, I see her as she must see me: pale, thin, tall-when-not-slouching. My platinum-dyed hair is growing in at the roots, which feels way too Courtney Love for this town. My shorts are torn, my legs are goosey, and the ample breasts I've been trying to hide my whole life in baggy shirts are tamped down today under a ratty old black t-shirt with a print of Escher's never-ending staircase. I bet I look anti-social. For the first time since high school graduation, I'm aware of being...the weird girl.

"But you look like an artist," Tara pronounces—and it doesn't actually sound like a critique, the way she says it. Which is not what I expected. "C'mon. There's plenty of space. I'll move some of my shit around, it's no big deal." Dismissing the issue as if it's settled, she dives back into the truck and slings one of my duffel bags over her other tanned shoulder. Without waiting for us to protest, she trots towards my new home. I follow, like a puppy.

Tara Rubenstein continues to surprise me. The second my Dad kisses me wetly on the cheek and turns the Gremlin back in the direction of my childhood home, my bizarre new roommate pulls an American Spirit from a silver case on her desk. She asks me with a look if I want one.

"I didn't think anyone in San Diego smoked anymore," I say, taking a cig gratefully. We smoked all the time in Savannah. It was just something the art kids were expected to do. Plus, smoking was a nice, built-in reason to take breaks during long sessions at the studio. In lieu of jamming a paint-brush through a canvas in a fit frustration, one could just take the sane way out and inhale some nicotine for a few minutes.

Tara arches a perfectly-tweezed eyebrow at me. "Thought you left all the hipsters behind at your old school, huh?"

"I dunno. It seems a little white-bread here. I guess I just expected..." I have no way to finish this sentence. Instead, I shrug at Tara, and direct a stream of smoke out of our window, in the direction of the quad.

The new dorm is more spacious than my digs in Savannah, though there's no private bathroom. Tara's clutter is draped over every surface on her side of our wide suite, but her mess is precise—exactly half of the area around the mini-fridge is covered with empty Miller Lites, just as exactly half the floor is covered with the kinds of bras I always assumed only existed for magazines—red, lacy, satiny things. I fold my arms over my chest.

"There are actually a lot of cool people," Tara says, her expression toggling between a grin and something more tense. It's like her programming won't accommodate a frown. "There's a decent music scene. A lot of the jocks are nice. And the best head of my life was a business school kid. Freshman. Last week."

"I thought you were with the RA?"

"And I thought you were from some fancy-ass cosmopolis?" Again, I wait for Tara to laugh with me, but she just smiles her weirdly forced smile again. "Here, art kid. Catch." I find myself ducking as a big rectangle flies right past my face, just about slicing my cheek. When I swivel and see what it is Tara's thrown at me, I laugh again. It's a big heavy hardback, titled *The Enlightened Orgasm.*

"Okay. We're gonna need to get started now to be at all timely for Halloween-in-July. You can unpack later." Tara stubs out her smoke and turns her focus to the sliding-door closet separating our twin beds. She immediately begins to yank things off hangers with abandon—ridiculous, glittery, patterned things that call to mind the dressing room of a Burlesque show. Like, a Burlesque show in 1985.

"Are you in the theatre department or something? Where'd you get all this?"

"Fashion merchandising. And I'm good at yard sales. Here." Tara's ponytail bobs back and forth as she marches across our room toward me, a big white garment in tow. I straighten as she holds the dress up to my frame, her muscular little arm extending high to adjust for our height difference. I marvel, again, at her shiny, efficient head. She's like a sassy robot.

"This should fit. So that just leaves your hair."

"I'm sorry, what? And also, where? Also—why?"

"Try to keep up, Savannah. The guys on Frat Row throw a big party for all the summer-school scumbags, and it's tonight. You want to land at SDU with a splash? Come out with us tonight, and look good."

"Dress-up isn't really my bag."

"Don't be coy. You have a killer figure and a pretty face. You're going to do just fine here." Tara begins to buzz around the room, like a fly. I give up on trying to predict her next move, and instead hug the white dress she's given me to my body and take a look at myself in the full-length closet mirror. I can't help but blush a little. Killer figure and pretty face? No one's ever said that to me before.

Tara reappears at my elbow, brandishing two cardboard boxes—each adorned with smiling women. At once, I put the pieces together.

"We'll just touch up your roots, and then you'll be the perfect Marilyn Monroe."

* * *

If Zooey could see me now.

But wait, of course she can! I pull my phone from its nest in my cleavage ("It's what Marilyn would have done," Tara claims) and take a pouty-face selfie. My lips are crimson red, my hair is freshly bleached, dyed, blow-dried and rolled, and the rest of me is powdered as it's never been powdered before. Tara kept me hostage in the bathroom for nearly an hour as she debated where to place Marilyn's trademark mole on my face. Together, we'd settled on the right side.

"I could still be Madonna. That feels a bit more me, to be honest." Tara'd just spent twenty minutes squeezing herself into a pleather catsuit, and was painting a slick line across each eyelid. "Don't be ridiculous," my new roommate told me. "Halloween is about being someone that's like, the opposite of you." I was so tickled by the incidental compliment—did Tara really think I wasn't the opposite of Madonna?—that I forgot to question her choice in going as Catwoman. So far, Tara had struck me as nothing so much as a sleek, savvy, sexual super-person. By her own logic, a crime-fighting vigilante didn't seem so far off.

Tara is suddenly at my side again, angling for more space in the full-length. She looks at me in my white, halter dress (suitable for subway grates) and smiles at her handiwork. For the first time all day, the grin seems genuine.

"Let's go raise some hell, Savannah," she says, turning so fast her cape snaps on my naked arms. "We're a couple of bad bitches." I laugh. The door of our dorm room closes with a final, frightening click behind us. Life at SDU, take one... I type across my selfie to Zo, as we stroll down the hallway. I imagine my best friend's face as she's confronted with my...froufy-ness. Hmm. I save the image, instead of sending it.

* * *

As we walk up Frat Row I start to feel giddy and nervous. The day has passed in such a whirlwind that I keep forgetting it's my first spent on a new campus—something about SDU's proximity to my childhood home makes me feel like less of a stranger, even though I'm definitely fresh meat. The architecture of all the buildings—faux adobe brick—is the same employed throughout my neighborhood. In high school, we used to take trips to SDU to visit the big library. And when Dad worked here, I was always having to wander around the quad as I waited for his shift to start or end. The college students today seem just as large and intimidating to me as they had then, when I was actually a kid.

Then again, I recognize faces. The kids who went to Carver Elementary, and then Blair Middle, Giuliani High—a good two thirds of these kids ended up at their state school. As I traipse through the night, self-conscious in my low-cut dress, it's like I'm flicking through an old yearbook: there's Sandy Dennys, the kid who, in sixth grade, got his jollies smacking his head against his desk until it bled. There's Shiloh Mueller, who brought in Creole food for International Day when we were eleven. And there's Gili VanHollen, the girl who threw up on Chase's shoes in the eighth grade during the MSA, and cried in his presence for years after the fact. And somewhere, hidden among the bougainvillea and textbooks and stoner kids and preppy kids, there's Chase Kelly in-the-flesh.

Not that I think I'm going to run into him. Thirty thousand other people go to this school. What are the odds?

I still don't know why he's plaguing me.

We saw each other almost every single day, for nine years. Even after he made Varsity baseball our sophomore year (unheard of at the time), our lockers were only three doors down. We smiled at each other every single day. Always said 'good morning.' Sometimes stopped for small-talk.

And at the beginning, of course, it was much more than that.

The day after that fateful mile, I became running buddies with Chase. We made a mockery of gym class, and Mr. Seidman ate it up. He gave us passes on all the easy stuff the uncoordinated kids were left to do (Wall Ball, Tetherball, Medicine Ball...) and let us jog around the soccer field during class, instead. One day, Chase even convinced Mr. S. to let us spend a class practicing "bending it like Beckham." That was a fun day.

Though I can't remember what class Brendan was supposed to be in during that period—it wasn't gym—he started hanging around, too. Not as athletic but smarter than both of us, Brendan liked to clench his fist into a ball and play "Commentator" while Chase and I played one on one. The smaller Kelly would always embroider his running remarks with a bunch of stupid jokes and puns, often at the expense of his golden brother. When Chase and I would get tired, we'd slump together around the base of the old oak tree at the edge of the playground, one place where the teachers would always forget to look. It was there that I received much of my "musical education," in the form of Brendan Kelly Original Mix CDS, made just for me. These had titles like, "Prog: An Odyssey" and, "Highway Driving, 101." (Never mind that I wasn't then old enough to drive, by a long shot.) We took turns passing around a beat-up Walkman and offering our thoughts on Brendan's "cool new tunes of the week." Often, Chase would get bored with this part of our day and leave Brendan and I to talk tunes while he shot hoops.

At one point, party lines were drawn. I started to get the hang of Brendan's zany jokes at the same time that Melora Handy and the other Ponytails were making it apparent to the whole fifth grade that it was high time every girl in a training bra had a public crush on a boy. Though the butterflies had abated after we'd become friends, I still had an echo of a crush on Chase; as I became better friends with Brendan, my falling for the jock-y twin began to feel inevitable. Even though, if I'm honest, I felt possessive about both of them. We were all so young.

"My brother likes you," Brendan told me one day while the two of us were passing The Velvet Underground back and forth, below the oak tree. I don't remember where Chase was.

"I like all three of us. We're musketeers."

"No, Avery. He really likes you. Like this." Then, Brendan had jammed his grimy foam headphones over my ears and turned the volume way, way up on "I'll Be Your Mirror."

"Chase doesn't even like The Velvet Underground," I'd said, blushing. But the seed that was planted on that first gym Friday had been watered. I'd since abandoned the possibility that my friendship with the Kellys could be more than platonic—but was it even a little possible that Chase could like me, the way Jeffy Kohan liked Corinne? It was a thrilling and strange proposition, this idea that my first-ever crush could actually love me in some new, adult way.

But we didn't discuss the matter further. Something about my response made Brendan clam up.

And on reflection, later, in the sanctum of my bedroom, I decided that was for the best. It was just too weird to talk to Brendan about my crush on his brother—even if we had become best friends. This exact line of thinking was why girls usually had friends who were girls, I would learn much later.

The three of us graduated elementary and proceeded to middle school, where two more years passed. Around us, girls grew breasts. Rumors circulated. We each held the monster off as long as we could, but on the very last day of eighth grade, I worked up the nerve. It was Field Day. Chase's hair, longer by then, framed his face—which was gathering manly definition and new angles with each passing day. It now seems insane to me that Chase Kelly made it through all three years of middle school (and one year of fifth grade) without once dating or kissing a girl. Maybe that had something to do with his single-minded athlete's focus.

There was this Trophy Party, for those of us who'd excelled in Field Day competitions—and Chase and I, go figure, presided over the distribution process like King and Queen. Right before the final game of the intramural soccer tournament I started in on the pump-up speech. You can do it, Avery, I murmured to the little faux gold athletes on their plastic plinths. Just turn to Chase and tell him you're in love with him. Say you've wanted to be more than friends for the past three years. Then you can spend the whole summer before high-school learning how to make out. You can tan in your two-piece while he— chiseled and golden, the natural yellows popping out his hair—can dance off the diving board every morning, and into your arms each night. (I was a dramatic kid. Sue me.)

"Chase," I started. But I was quiet, and he didn't hear me. "Chase," I repeated. "Can we talk for a sec?"

It was at that moment that the Ponytails rushed toward the trophy table, giggling.

"I can't believe we still have a Field Day," Carrie Lundergaard was saying. "That's, like, so elementary."

I was still angling for Chase's attention, ever clueless, when the little crowd parted and Melora Handy stepped forward, like something out of a fairy tale. She was always getting these trendy haircuts—her mom was a stylist—and today she'd elected to honor our mini-Olympics with a throwback: kinked hair.

It should have been clear to me earlier. He was one of my two best friends at that school. But I had to see it to believe it. As Melora came toward us, I watched Chase turn into a soggy, sweaty ball of pheromones. I watched him puff out his chest and set his jaw in that ironic way I liked, before flicking his hair like he just didn't care. And Melora appeared to bloom in his presence. She threw her mane back and laughed at nothing, pushing her breasts forward like she was someone's older sister. I remember thinking, even then, that it was all so stupid—the pageantry our culture demanded, this coyness about who liked who and how they showed it—but more importantly, that day I saw, firsthand, how some people look made for each other, and others don't.

I never told Chase about my crush. Four days later, I walked in on him with one hand up a Ponytail's shirt in the girl's locker room at the public pool. As if I needed further confirmation: Chase Kelly wanted to be no one's "mirror" but Melora Handy's.

I spent the summer and some of the fall trading tapes and records with Brendan, who never again pressed me about liking his brother. A few months into freshman year, I fell in with a more high-school appropriate clique of perturbed, smart, artsy girls who would become my surrogate family before fleeing to the East Coast for college. It's weird. You'd really think one could leave it at that. All this stuff happened so long ago. Since I had a monstrous crush on Chase, I've told other men I loved them (Gary Pinter, junior year prom) and lost my virginity (see previous). In Savannah, I did my fair share of freshman experimenting—before, of course, my world came crashing down around my ears—but how is it that I could still be so titillated by the mere memory of that boy? Those twins? I take a drag of Tara's American Spirit, letting the acrid smoke fill up my lungs. I guess you never forget your first.

"Et voila!" Tara finally hollers, clicking her leather boots together at the heels like she's a dictator. "Welcome to Halloween-in-July, newbie. Let's get our freak on."

Chapter Three

* * *

Mama Rubenstein leads me through a crowded labyrinth of costumed co-eds, and I mean literally: she takes my hand in hers.

"Don't drink out of anything!" my new roommate hollers at me, half-joking. But my stomach drops. I feel a wave of nausea envelope my body, like that fateful breeze did Marilyn in The Seven Year Itch. Even the joke possibility of being roofied sends me straight back to the night in Savannah. I'm suddenly cold.

"Fresh meat?" someone cries from over my shoulder. The voice belongs to a boy, but when I turn, I see an elegantly made up Glinda the Good Witch, in all her glittering finery. Tara bares her teeth.

"And who the fuck are you supposed to be?"

"I could ask you the same question, bitch. Does Gothika know you've been raiding her wardrobe?"

"Fuck you, Princess—Peach?"

"She's Glinda!" I offer, proud of myself. The Good Witch smiles at me.

"Trevor, meet my new roomie. Savannah."

"It's Avery, actually," I correct, though Tara shoots Trevor a look like I'm her toddler and I've just informed everyone I'll be living on the moon from now on. I decide to let this go.

"Trevor, is it? So nice to meet you. Your costume is beautiful."

"Thanks, Marilyn. But it's you who takes the cake this evening. You've got the hair right and everything." Trevor the Good Witch reaches out to cup one of my peroxide-perfect curls, and I can't help but blush.

"She's as lovely as the real thing, too. Perfect. Okay," I notice that Trevor changes subjects as efficiently as Tara. "Let me get you two ladies cocktails."

"That would be magical," Tara sneer-grins.

We don't wait for Trevor to return with whatever a 'cocktail' would be at this motley event; rather, Tara drags us further into the frat house. So far, Casa Delta Nu is as fratty as Savannah was hip. Lots of girls in nurse and French maid costumes. Sexy kittens. Sexy witches. When each one we pass shoots me the same steely glance that's half intrigued, half hateful, I'm reminded that I, of course, am dressed just like everyone else here. Which is to say—dressed to impress a guy.

Tara says hey to a few more people. Most are men. We shuffle and shuffle through the stuffed corridors. Finally, my guide throws up her hands.

"Fuck," Tara groans, planting her feet in a little turreted window space that's separated from the rest of the party. For the first time, my fearless leader appears to be taking a rest. She draws an American Spirit from some snug fold in the cleavage of her catsuit.

"Should I try to find Trevor?" Across the hall, a Ronald McDonald and a Snooki enter into a screaming match. A guy in a big Ketchup bottle takes a short tumble down the stairs.

"Nah. He's probably found Zeke by now." I can't help but love how Tara talks to me like we've been friends for years already, assuming I know everyone. Then again, maybe I do—for here comes Tatiana Brewster, from my tenth grade Pre-Calc class. She giggles as she tries to re-fasten the top buttons of her I-wanna-say flight attendant's costume.

"This party is a total bust."

Tara doesn't seem to need me to respond, so I just nod. Tatiana starts to peer at me across the landing, at the same time Tara offers me the stubby part of her half-vanished smoke. Though I'm not used to this much tobacco in a single day, I take it.

"What high-school did you say you went to again?" I ask Tara, pivoting my body out of Tatiana's eye-line. I so don't want a catch-up session right now, though the latter continues to peer at me. It's getting creepy.

"You wouldn't know it. It's out of state."

"You came to SDU from out of state?!"

Tara's eyes flash with anger. Her smile escapes. "I'm from Wyoming, and I like the beach. It's not so weird."

"OH. MY. GOD. IT'S YOU!" Fuck. I'd recognize that designer-imposter perfume anywhere. I turn, and find myself smothered in a cloud of Brewster's D-Cups and l'eau d'Baby Prostitute. Also, a touch of Bud Light Lime.

"Angry Avery! We never expected to see you again!" Tatiana gushes, like we're the oldest of friends. As if there's anyone standing next to her, made complicit in her 'we.' "Didn't you get some fancy-ass scholarship to dance school, or something? In Canada?"

"Art school. In Georgia. But I've transferred home for the fall semester."

Tatiana frowns, in a way reminiscent of every single day in our Pre-Calc class.

"Why'd you do that?" she pouts. My face grows hot again. I feel Tara's gaze, penetrative and curious. Looking for something to do, I let my eyes scan the rooms around our turret.

And that's when I see him.

My first impulse trumps the docile, Marilyn voice inside my head—the one that's screaming, "Play coy! Wait for his jaw to drop!" Instead, I rise with my heartbeat and hustle into the room Tatiana's just vacated. "You hottie with a body!" I shriek, punching Brendan Kelly hard on the shoulder. It's like the cocktail I never received has made me ultra-bold. Perhaps it's just the opportune timing.

At first, my old friend recoils, a look of bemusement crossing his perfect features—but I delight in watching recognition sweep over his face. I take his epiphany moment to look him up and down. It's only been a year since I saw him last, but the changes begun in high-school have clearly continued.

For starters, there's the lip ring. The thin silver hoop he used to wear in one ear has apparently migrated south on Brendan's face. He's dressed the same—obscure, ratty band T, dark jeans to hide the stains, Converses—but his body looks different. More athletic, less scrawny. He's been working out.

"Hey, girl," Brendan responds, opening his bulging arms wide and pulling me into an aromatic bear hug. Which is a little weird, since the Brendan I know never wore cologne. I brush against the taut muscles of his stomach, and feel my face flush.

His hair is shorter, too. He's wearing it high and tight, though there's just enough length that a few tendrils fall across his face and catch the light. He flicks these away with an endearing swipe of his hand.

"Angry Avery is transferring here," Tatiana says, having appeared in the doorframe. Tara trots up in her wake.

"Hey, Savannah—why'd they call you Angry Avery?"

"Because she told off a math teacher–"

"ONE time!"

"For being sexist as shit," Brendan laughs, and his voice is lighter than I remember it. It lacks that stoner-y, fried sound that I actually used to find a little sexy.

"I hate that 'girls-can't-do-math' bullshit. Ugh." I push a blonde curl behind my ear, but let it lie when it promptly falls back across my face. Who am I trying to impress? It's just Brendan.

"Seriously, Mr. Kelly. I am so glad to see you. Oh, man—can we hang out? I want to know everything! My Dad mentioned your band is on the radio? That's so awesome!"

"It's pretty cool, yeah."

"Savannah, you never told me you had a hot high-school friend in Delta Nu!" Tara has pushed her way past Tatiana, who looks a little put out to be abandoned in the door-frame.

I look at Brendan, who's grinning in that wry way I associate more with his brother. This room is not well-lit, but a stripe of moonlight brightens Brendan's forehead, his dark eyebrows, his greyish-green eyes. I color a little. Okay, he is attractive. He's an attractive, attractive man. But that's always been true. We're old friends. Nothing is different now.

"We haven't been good friends in a long time, actually," Brendan says. "But I've missed Angry Avery a whole big lot." His eyes flick down, so fast I don't quite catch his drift. But the other two girls in the room shift uncomfortably in their teetering shoes. Brendan Kelly definitely just scoped my tits.

Which, to be fair, are on pretty bold display this evening.

"I've missed you, too, J.K." I say, punching Brendan on the shoulder. "Look at you. Staying out of jail and everything. I'm so proud."

Brendan rubs the patch of his (round, smooth...) bicep where I've slugged him. He's making a strange face, I notice. Like a grimacing, constipated face.

"Did I actually hurt you?" I ask, affecting worry. I mean, there's no way. It was a tap. God, he looks cute when he bites his lip like that. And that windswept, rock star hair. Fuck.

Brendan looks at Tatiana, who's suddenly got the same expression on her heavily made-up face. Tara, unamused, shifts her weight and gives me a look I can interpret, easily: Piss, or get off the pot.

"Do you want to tell her?" Tatiana asks. Her voice breaks as she speaks. When I turn back to Brendan, his screwy expression has broken open into an easy grin. A familiar grin. I get it before he even tells me.

"Avery, I'm Chase," the boy in front of me stutters. To demonstrate his good faith, he lifts the little silver hoop easily out of his lip. "It's for Halloween, you know. I'm supposed to be Brendan." As if he's anticipating an Angry girl swipe, Chase Kelly grabs my hand. His grip—warm and slightly moist—is a whole continent of memories unto itself. His light green eyes, the ones I used to gaze into, below the old oak tree, are full of compassion.

How could I not have known?

"But hey. I am really, really happy to see you." Then, the flicker happens again, and this time there's no doubt about it. Chase Kelly is staring at my breasts.

Trevor barrels into the upstairs bedroom just moments after the Big Reveal. The abrupt change of scenery feels appropriate, for I desperately need to recalibrate. It immediately seems wrong that I'd punched Chase Kelly on the shoulder. After the pool locker room incident in eighth grade, I'd never been as physically close with Chase as I had been with his brother. The last time I joke-punched him, I was probably eleven years old.

"You ass," I mutter, in a new and smaller voice.

"I'm sorry. I couldn't help it."

Tatiana was leaning against the wall, she was laughing so hard. Chase was smirking that ironic smile he'd maintained, apparently, since the first day we met. And it was then that everything in the room really seemed to change. It was happening. Me and Chase, adults, reconnecting, in a room. I was older, now. I could do everything Melora had.

Tara took the hint, dragging Trevor back out of the bedroom and towards the hallway. They must have picked up Tatiana on the way, because the next thing I know, I'm alone with Chase. He leans back on his ottoman and reaches for a beer resting on the mantelpiece. He looks me up and down again. This time, his eyes on my skin give me goosebumps.

"Seriously, I'm sorry, Angry Avery. It was too good a test to pass up. Our oldest childhood friend can't even tell us apart!" Chase takes a slug of his beer, and I watch his throat rise and fall as he swallows. Something tells me to lean forward from my perch on the edge of the bed. Just enough, so he can see me.

"You said it yourself, bud. We haven't exactly been friends in a long time."

"What's that they say? Bygones, be bygones." Chase takes another swallow, before offering me his beer-can with a gesture. I reach for it, even though I'm not thirsty. When he leans forward, our fingers brush.

"Now that you're an SDU gal, we can start over from scratch. You still like to run?"

My heart flips. He remembered.

"I still like to run, sure. Laps. Around you." I wait for Chase to laugh at my shitty pun, but instead he just smiles vaguely as his eyes plummet back toward my neckline.

"My brother'll be glad to see you. You and him always had—well, you guys were close, right?"

"Before Mary Jane got him, sure."

Chase furrows his brow. "Who's Mary Jane?"

The moonlight moves behind some trees, letting the room lapse into a comfortable darkness. In the dim light, it's easier to pretend we're kids again. Just two souls who'd connected, once upon a time, under a tree.

"Listen, Angry Avery," Chase starts, his voice low and gravelly, like his brother's. I lean farther forward, until I can feel the air moving around his mouth as he speaks. His breath comes fast, and it smells sweet...

I let out a yelp, as his hand grazes my knee through the thin satin of my dress. I stand and move quickly toward the window, unsure how to feel about what's happening.

"You look so beautiful, dressed up like that." Chase rises behind me, and I see more of his college boy bod, and what a mockery it makes of his "Brendan" costume. His tall stance seems at odds with the Daniel Johnston t-shirt. His muscular legs appear strained in the skinny jeans. My gaze drifts downward, without my consent. Even in the moonlight, I can see how the denim contours his package. On thinking this, I have to turn away again.

"You've changed a lot since high-school. I can tell." He walks towards me, his gait somehow familiar and strange all at once. "You're more confident. I dig it."

I keep my gaze focused on the activity outside Delta Nu, the coeds moving around on the lawn below. It's surreal, to be standing here in this room, dressed as a princess, pursued by a prince. Suddenly his hands find my hips...

"There's no chance you'd wanna—go somewhere and really catch up, right?" The pads of Chase's fingers find my hip-bones, and at first they tread lightly. If anyone were to walk in right now, we might still look innocent, standing there in the window's profile. But slowly, like molasses, Chase pours more movement into his fingertips. He massages me slightly, and I feel myself open at the joints; my knees begin to part, involuntarily.

"Not tonight," I say quickly, as blood rises up from my chest and into my face. I duck my head, so Chase can't see me looking totally fifteen and goofy. When we'd locked eyes—in the glass of the windowpane, before I leapt away from him and towards the door—I did feel something. Sure, he had the unabashed look of a more-than-buzzed guy at a frat party, but I swear a stronger sensation moved between us. It's still lingering.

"Totally understand," Chase says, after a heartbeat. "But take my number. Just in case."

"Why?"

"Because I'd like to take you out." And there was that famous Kelly smirk again, in all its glory. The face that had brought me to my knees ten years prior. I fish in my cleavage, beet-red, before procuring my iPhone. I wait patiently for him to plug his digits in, and then I turn, the picture of almost-cool, and follow my two new amigos to a diner.

Chapter Four

* * *

"Tell me again why you didn't go home with the ripped reincarnation of Kurt Cobain back there?" Trevor asks, his lipstick smearing across the sesame bun of his black bean burger. We're at the least popular of the three diners closest to campus, and the 'we' I refer to is the strike-out-crew—Trevor, Tara and me.

"I'm trying this new thing where I don't jump into the sack with randos." Above my head, Trev and Tara exchange arch looks, and in the interest of not being a judgmental ass, I backpedal. "Not that casual sex is bad." *All the time*, I don't add.

"But it's not like you just met him. Haven't you known this guy for years?"

"I'd do him." Tara sprinkles some table salt into her palm, for no discernible reason. "In an airplane. In a phone booth. On a roof..."

"Who are you, Dirty Dr. Seuss?"

My roommate sips some of her Diet Dr. Pepper, smiling tautly. She didn't order any food.

"It's also a little weird, right? That he dressed up as his twin for Halloween? And pranked me about it?"

"What are you talking about? It's fucking hilarious," Tara says, without laughing.

"I was only looking at his arms, TBH," Trevor sighs. He sets his burger down, and cocks his head so the Glinda wig slides sideways.

Trevor catches the Glinda wig before it goes sailing into the ketchup, ripping the sparkly thing off his head with no small irritation. Underneath, I'm surprised to see that my new friend is bald.

"Your phone is blowing up, lady," Tara says, as she extracts a single french fry from the tangle on Trevor's plate. My heart does a backflip. I've got three new messages, but my fingers are too sweaty to scroll.

The first two are from Zooey, demanding to know how my first night went. But I skip past those in favor of the newest addition to my paltry list of contacts: Mr. Perfect. Like, he actually named himself Mr. Perfect in my phone.

Asshole, I think—though I smile to myself as I read:

"Still think you can run laps around me, Angry A?"

"Yes," I manage, deciding not to comment on his drunk "speech." That probably wouldn't be cute.

"Good. Tomorrow morning. Let's go for a run. Meet me at the old oak tree by the science building, 1130am. Sound good?"

I knew it. I knew it was worth it, to wait.

"Yes," I type again. For a second, I worry that my speediness screams 'eager beaver'—but then, Mr. Perfect sends an emoji of a sleeping cat.

I have a date.

On my first day at school.

With the first boy I ever loved.

Who said San Diego was so bad?

Chapter Five

* * *

I wake up at eight, feeling fresh-faced and thrilled despite the four hours of sleep. Across the room, Tara snores deeply, a satin eye-mask covering most of her face. Cuddled up beside her on the narrow twin bed is Trevor, who apparently crashed at ours last night. His Glinda make-up is smudged something fierce.

Careful not to wake new-roomie and surrogate-roomie, I press my feet to the cold tile and make for my many unpacked bags, which have been abandoned in a heap by the front door. I need to (stealthily) find my running gear, and not just any running gear—the sexy, Lycra stuff. Back in Savannah, I preferred to go for morning runs in the uniform of a harried Dad: grey sweatpants and a billowy white t-shirt were par for my course. Last year, though, Zooey had given me a gift certificate to LuluLemon—which was her idea of an inside joke, given all those hours we spent playing Camel Toe Hunt like assholes. I'd splurged on some high-quality gear—booty shorts and sports bras—and naturally, never found a need to shake up my style. But this run is like the ball. If Brendan Kelly got an eyeful of the Cinderell-ized version of his old pal last night, I want to show him that the genuine article can be just as foxy without the pearls and lipstick.

But wait—not Brendan. Chase, dressed as Brendan. I shake my head at the mental mistake, sliding one leg first into the snug pants. God damn, these are tight. But I keep my eye on the prize: Chase, Chase, Chase....

Visions from last night bob to the top of my memory: Chase's sexy-ass lip-ring (though, of course, that had been a joke), Chase's brooding demeanor (though, of course, that had been a costume), Chase's body, carved like a Rodin figure (sigh...the real thing). My stomach flips again with anticipation. I shake the urge to text him, just to make sure everything really happened last night—but something tells me to do so would be super needy. Instead, I turn my focus to the impossible-seeming task of unpacking. I ease my duffel bag open, and find myself faced with a horror story: it's the floral, baby-doll dress I was wearing on that horrible night in Savannah. Why, oh why, did I keep this thing?

My heart starts pounding against my rib-cage, and I feel angry tears begin to swim below my eyelids. Yes, angry—and maybe I will always be Angry Avery, in my way. I hastily look over to Tara and Trevor, just to make sure they're still asleep, the way I did so many mornings in Georgia when I didn't want Zooey to catch me crying. That monster. It makes me so furious that the memory of him can still scare me, even when he's thousands of miles away.

It's then that my phone buzzes with a welcome distraction: "I know it's early, but I couldn't sleep. Any chance ur awake? Got a protein shake with your name on it if so."

I brush the rumblings of my tears away, and feel my heart ping-pong back towards glee. I'm going out with a good guy today. Everything is going to be different in this city. I stand, I stretch, I type back:

"Meetcha at the tree in ten?"

* * *

"I can't believe you don't remember the treehouse!"

"I remember a fort. We didn't build anything in a tree."

"But we definitely called it a Tree House. Because it was inspired by those doofy books your brother used to be obsessed with. Remember?"

"The Magic Treehouse."

"Yes!"

"Ever the egg-head, that Brendan."

"Remember when your mother said we could practice tie-dye with her wedding dress? That was what we used as a curtain! I'm actually shocked at how well I'm able to remember some of this stuff." I bend low for a stretch, pausing to squint up at Chase from the ground. He's still leaning against the oak tree, clutching the protein shake. In his Top Gun aviators and Letterman jacket, he doesn't exactly look ready for a good sprint around campus. I remain unsure as to whether or not we're really going to get any running done this morning.

"Right. Right. That was so fucked up." Chase appears lost in thought for a moment, but then his eyes fall back to me. The grin he shoots me sends a shiver up my spine— it's the exact same one I remember from our mile-running days.

"This is nice," I say, pulling myself out of a lunge. "It feels like old times, doesn't it?" At last, Chase takes off his jacket, as if to disprove this remark with the contents below: his biceps ripple out from beneath a ribbed wife beater, so rounded and taut that my eyes bulge. He's so jacked he stands just shy of early Sylvester Stallone territory—even the tendons in his neck stand out. Chase's skin appears golden in the early morning sun, and I can see the highlights in his hair in a way I didn't notice at the party last night. Yeah, Avery, it's just like old times. Except your Spongebob-loving ex-BFF is a body-builder now. And I'm pretty sure those sun-streaks are dyed in.

Instead of responding, Chase just smiles—and the impish way he does so makes it clear that he's caught my awed expression. Pushing the glasses up to perch on his head, he extends a huge foot toward the base of the oak tree, lazily stretching a hamstring. When he bends down, a tendril of his blonde hair falls out from behind the aviators, and he attempts to blow this away.

"Wanna hold my feet while I do some sit-ups?" Chase says, flopping suddenly to the ground. I'm gazing at his Herculean figure so hard that I almost forget to nod. Crouching before him, I press my palms into the tops of his feet. His crotch is right there in front of me, splayed and ready—oh, my God. I have to look up at the sky instead.

Chase starts to grunt as he pulls himself forward with each sit-up. As I watch all the musculature in his arms and legs flex with effort, I feel like I'm watching ballet. He really is a beautiful boy. The fine hair along his legs is like dust—it's more golden than he is, nearly opaque. His movements are so fluid it's clear that there's a six-pack lurking underneath that wife-beater. I want to rest my head against it. I want to hear his muscles thrum and churn.

I hear girl-voices across the quad, and yank my eyes from the perfect body in front of me just in time to catch three leggy brunettes scurrying away like they've been caught.

"Did you know them?" I ask Chase. "Oh—err, thirty-two..."

"Probably just the fan-club," Chase wheezes. "Thirty-three." Sweat begins to rise in a line along his forehead, darkening his blonde hair.

"You're kidding."

Chase collapses against the dust, dramatically. He peers up at me, between rigorous exhales, and pulls an adorable shrug face.

"Oh come on, Kelly! I'm sure the ladies of SDU don't just flock to see you work out. You're so vain, you probably think this song is about you."

Chase arches an eyebrow. "What song?"

"You know, the song. Carly Simon?"

"Does she go here, or something?" Chase pulls himself up to sitting, indicating I can finally release my grip on his big feet. I bite my lip, trying not to be the asshole. I guess it's not that weird. Plenty of people don't know who Carly Simon is. She's pretty old-school.

"You feel like running yet, Angry Avery?"

"Oh, I've been ready. I was born ready." Chase smiles at me, in a way that shows his teeth. I watch an impulse cross his face, and before I know it, he's fallen back to the ground again and grabbed hold of my hands. He kicks off his sneakers, then draws me forward, up the length of his torso, so my own stomach comes to rest on the soles of his feet. I let out an involuntarily terror-giggle.

"Just relax. And think about extending from every limb."

"Ahhh—Chase, your feet are dirty! And cold!"

He doesn't say anything, but gazes into my eyes as he begins to extend his legs, slowly at first. His thighs and arms quiver with the effort of supporting me. I try not to laugh again, even though I'm not thrilled about being yanked into some weird new couples' stretch without being asked first.

"Look up!" Chase urges, gesturing with his chin. I let myself abandon his wide, green eyes and scan the horizon. For a second, it is like levitation. That is, until I stop to consider Chase's view from below—the low-hanging cleavage and all.

"Brendan! Brendan, I'm flying!" I giggle. At this, Chase frowns a little, then slowly lowers his knees until I can find footing on the ground again. "It's Chase, remember."

But before I can explain my ostensibly obvious Titanic joke, Chase has shaken off his minor irritation. I see in him something like Tara's single-mindedness, that ability to switch gears rapidly and remain intense. Maybe they're birds of a feather. Or maybe everyone in San Diego is just like that.

Hopping to his feet, the golden Kelly starts to bounce on his toes. "Now let's see if you can still lap me, girl," he smiles. He wiggles his eyebrows at me, and I feel his irises scan my frame. I blush hard when he lingers on my curves, and turn my gaze to the quad. Before Chase can count us off or set a course, I start to run.

Chapter Six

* * *

Tara pours a third Splenda into her Diet Dr. Pepper (don't ask me), and peers at me over the tops of her dark, ridiculous, Lady Gaga-esque sunglasses. The dorm room is pretty much exactly as I left it.

"I can't believe you already went on a date, bitch. You literally haven't even unpacked yet. And it's like noon on a Sunday."

"It's like, four," I say, slowly squeezing more of the moisture out of my hair. "And I'm not even sure that was a date. It was more like a high-school reunion." Tara snorts, and I let my eyes close for a second. Okay, okay, it was a date. I know it was a date because "high-school reunions" don't typically end with one person asking the other to take a shower with them.

We'd been sweaty and exhausted. As determined as ever to prove my mettle to Chase, I'd elected to push myself way past any exercise limits established in recent training. We'd looped the whole campus twice, pausing to chug Gatorade outside the old Science building, the

Student Union, and finally, Dresher Hall. "If you squint from this point, you can see the ocean," Chase had said. "Highest ground on campus." Then he'd pointed, and I'd followed his finger to the wide, shimmering Pacific. "This also happens to be my dorm room," my running buddy finished. And just then, I'd gotten the feeling that I'd been brought here with an agenda.

"I thought you lived with the Delta Nu guys."

"Those clowns? Nah. I have a single on the third floor. It's very quiet. Big windows. At the end of the hall." I'd been aware of Chase's damp body coming closer to mine, the approach of his sharp, sweet smell. He'd put an experimental palm on my waist, squeezed me for a moment around the abdomen. We weren't moving, but his breath was beginning to come faster.

"You look really hot in this. Did I tell you that before?"

"What, my running gear? You liar."

"And you looked really, really hot in that dress last night." The intensity of his gaze had demanded eye contact, so I forgot about the ocean moving distantly below us. Chase came even closer, so our hip bones were touching. The hand he'd wrapped around my middle squeezed me gently.

"I borrowed that dress from Tara," I managed to choke out, suave as ever. Chase smiled. For the first time, I saw a dimple appear in his face—just one, on the left side of his mouth. Unthinkingly, I moved a finger up to his strong chin. I pressed into the small cleft.

"You have gotten very handsome," I whispered, shocked at my own confidence. This was the attitude of some sexier woman, no one I recognized. Someone like Tara could tell a man he was handsome, but not me.

"And you are fucking sexy," Chase growled, biting his lip. I hadn't even realized our closing proximity, but we were so close by then that I was aware then of his racing heartbeat. I let myself sink a little farther into his arms. We were both sticky and sweaty. What did it matter?

"I want to scrub you down," Chase murmured, bending low so he could speak into my ear. "How does that sound, Angry A? I want to put you in a shower and watch the water run off those beautiful breasts." His lips connected with my ear, lightly at first, before I felt the gentle pressure of his teeth on my cartilage. I leaned into him.

"I'm not really the kind of girl who suds up with a man on a first date," I murmured back, surprising myself again. Chase's hand had grown more urgent around my waist. His fingers flexed and pressed against my sore muscles.

"It's not really our first date, though. I'd say we've been seeing one another at regular intervals for a good ten years." His lips moved down to my neck, where they lingered, expelling air for a moment in a cool stream. "High time."

It would have been easy.

I could have let his strong, serious hands continue their journey across my flesh, finding my crevices, exploring my tender patches. We were in broad daylight, but it hadn't seemed to matter. There was no Kelly Fan Club around, to infringe on our privacy. There was only the distant sound of the ocean, and the closer-by sound of birds chirping in the live oaks. In another life, I would have let him back me up against a tree and kiss me, the way I'd always wanted him to kiss me. He would have tilted my head back gently, his eyes pausing to scan my face. He'd acknowledge our past together in a look—an expression fraught with all our mutual pain and panic, all those conversations on the playground discussing our parents, our futures. We'd been lonely together, but he'd kiss me, and in that one moment of connection it'd be clear that we'd never be lonely again. We'd be one body.

In real life, though, I'd let him nuzzle the space below my ear for a moment longer before backing away. I'd told him I had to go unpack. I'd been very nearly sucked back by the flummoxed expression on his face, the smoothness of his skin as he continued to draw patterns on my body with his fingers—but in the end, I'd jogged back to the dorm. I'd grabbed my shower gear, checked under each stall in the community bathroom, and on stepping into the stall let my imagination take hold. With the help of my trusty, pink, thankfully-waterproof vibrator, I'd touched myself, and experienced in my head what I'd been too afraid to experience up close. Chase Kelly's hands on my nakedness. Chase Kelly's animal thrusts into my pulsing wetness...

"So why didn't you seal the deal?!" Tara demands, mind-reader that she is. I wonder if my face is glowing from that little bathroom tryst.

"Ehh. Gotta preserve a little mystery, right?" I shake my hair out to make it seem like this remark comes off the cuff, and Tara appears satisfied—though she shakes her own matted head, taking a slug of her gross Dr. Pepper.

"I don't get you, Savannah. Life is short, you know."

The real truth? It hadn't felt right. I figure I've been waiting for Chase Kelly since I was eleven years old, why should I give it all away on the first day of our reconnection? What's the harm in doing this like a lady? Add to that the fact of my fear—that miserable shadow. As soon as I'd come back to the dorm, I'd balled up the floral dress and thrown it down the garbage chute. Fuck that guy for trying to destroy my future, as well as my past. I refuse to let him haunt me.

"On the other hand," Tara drawls, finally lurching out of her nest. (Trevor apparently flew the coop sometime during my non-date.) "He really didn't get the Titanic thing? Because this makes me worry he's an idiot."

When I look up at my roomie, she's smiling her bright, constructed smile—but I catch a glint of an eyebrow over her ridiculous sunglasses. I laugh with her, feeling only a little bit bad.

* * *

Fun fact: the week before summer session starts at SDU is called "Fuhgettaboutit," because everyone is supposed to be drinking themselves into a black-out state every night. My poor old Pa did not seem to realize this when he dropped me off two days ago, claiming that I "should try to get there early. Meet the summer school kids. Learn where the library is, and whatnot."

Library, schmi-brary. Tara Rubenstein has other plans in mind.

Around six p.m., she rallies, jerking herself from a Netflix binge-ing, hungover haze. I still haven't seen my roommate eat anything but Diet Dr. Pepper, a single french fry and water, which of course could explain her ability to slide into catsuits with ease. I've spent the late afternoon actually unpacking, though I'm so distracted it's hard to be precise. Like, I already forget where I've put all my socks. Then again, I'm distracted by many floating hypotheticals:

Did I make a mistake, not going off to shower with Chase? Have I blown it? Will he ever talk to me again? I want to bug Tara, but it's not like we're actual best friends yet—she could get annoyed with the pesky girl talk. It's then, with a pang, that I remember Zooey, and her thirty unanswered text messages.

"Oh my God! Hi!" She answers on the second ring. "I worried you died or something!"

"No, the opposite! Hey, you!" Her voice sounds so far away. Which, of course, makes perfect sense. She is.

"Hey, you! Man! How is school?"

"Hasn't started yet. But the campus is pretty." I glance back into the dorm room, having left the door ajar. Tara is smoking an American Spirit out the window, gazing intently at something (or, more likely, some one) on the green.

"Is it all jocks and hippies and Camel Toes? Are you living in *Clueless*?" My best friend laughs, but my first impulse is to defend my new turf.

"It's not that bad, actually. My roommate is really great. And there's this guy, Trevor—he's pretty cool."

"You already met a guy? Damn, California. They sure work fast out West."

"Trevor's gay."

"Oh. Sorry, I shouldn't have assumed." There's a beat of silence on the line, which I decide is filled with tension. Why are we being so weird with one another?

"How's Georgia?"

"Still shitty. But it misses you." I feel like I can hear Zooey's mood lift; her tone changes. "There's a new Studio Manager, actually. This chick named Magnus, from Ireland. She's actually a really inspired multi-medium print-maker—she does these Bearden-like cut-out arrangements on canvas, and then paints these lurid

Kandinsky scenes on top of them, in pastel. They're really busy pieces but very arresting. I think we're going to–"

Inside the dorm room, I spy Tara extinguishing her cigarette on the sill, and turning her gaze to the closet. She commences the same ritual from last night: pulling dresses and slips and shoes off the racks, assessing these in the mirror, then throwing them onto the floor in little piles. If I didn't know any better, I'd say crazy is planning to go out again.

"...so, that's an exciting new development. Not that I ever went in for Student Government, but it would be nice to take an active role in things like our dispensation for art supplies. You know?"

"Right. Definitely. She sounds great!" Silence on the line, then Zooey lets out an exhausted-sounding sigh.

"You didn't catch all of that, did you?"

"No, I'm sorry, Zo. I got distracted."

"See something shiny? Some, like, totally cool accessory?"

"Oh ha, ha." Tara's face materializes in the doorway. Shockingly, she's already applied a perfect face of make-up—even though it seems like she was in bed ten minutes ago.

"Hey bitch, there's a show tonight at the Ruby Room. Can you be ready in ten?" She pulls a face at my phone, but it's not an apologetic one. I cover the mouthpiece.

"I don't have a fake, though."

"Doesn't matter. RA Jeff is gonna get us in."

"Is that—the RA?"

Tara just grins her maniacal grin, which I take for a yes. The idea of spending another night in the wake of this adventure-loving pixie is too good to pass up.

"Hey—Zooey?"

"Oh my GOD. Who was that?"

"My roommate. Listen..."

"You actually let her call you 'bitch'? Oh my God, can you send me a picture of this Regina George?"

"She's actually really cool. Listen. I have to go."

There's some more silence on the line, during which I can perfectly picture Zooey's face. I've never stood up to— well, more like deliberately agitated—my best friend before. Not that I'm some big pushover or anything, but that's just never been our dynamic. In my mind's eye, my old buddy is shocked, her eyebrows raised and joined in an echo of Vivien Leigh. Very Savannah.

"Have fun with your new girlfriends!" Zo says, over-pronouncing the last word so it comes out mocking. Inside our room, Tara points to an invisible watch. Rolling my eyes, I make my decision. The iPhone clicks off, and the heels click on.

"I think you'd rock the shit out of this thing," Tara says, starting a conversation in the middle. "I'm too short for it." It's like she doesn't believe I brought any of my own clothes to college. I begin to protest, but then the dress materializes in the mirror. It's this funky old paisley print, with a cinched bodice, flared mini A-line skirt, and long, droopy bell-bottom sleeves. This dress looks like something Janis Joplin might have worn on a third date. All I need is a boa.

"Good, right? Last year the school did Hair, and I was boning a guy in the orchestra pit." Tara's already half into her own nod to retro: a mod, black and white mini-dress that hugs her form tightly. She clips on a pair of globular enamel earrings to complete the effect, before appraising me. I love this dress. It fits me like a glove, it's comfortable, and it's sexy. I feel way more myself in this get-up than I did in the Marilyn costume.

"Nice," Tara allows, before smearing a line of black lipstick across her pout. I'm fluffing my hair—which is remarkably Courtney Love, post-shower—when there's a knock at the door. Tara hustles over to admit a gangly black guy with frameless eyeglasses and a smooth, shaved head. He's wearing a button down white-shirt, dark jeans, and a vest. Of all things.

"Just popping by to say hey to the new blood," the stranger says, smiling without showing his teeth. Meanwhile, Tara rolls her eyes as she jams one foot into a white pleather knee-high boot. "I'm RA Jeff, but the ladies call me Jeffrey. And you're?"

"Avery Lynne."

"Transfer?"

"Yeah. But I grew up around here, actually." RA Jeff appears half-interested in my answers at best—his gaze is pinned to Tara's wiggling ass, as she fusses with her second pleather boot. The way he drifts around our dorm room makes me certain he's spent a lot of time in here. He locates my roomie's sleek cigarette case, for instance, without even feigning to look for it.

"Baby doll, you're really gonna wear that? It's not exactly subtle." RA Jeff murmurs to Tara like they're alone, so I resume getting made up in the mirror. I have to admit: dolling up for an adventure like this is really fun. I wish I'd gone out into the city more, in Savannah.

"I know you didn't just tell me I don't look fabulous."
At this, RA Jeff backs off. Something in Tara's eyes makes
our resident advisor retreat all the way to the hallway.

"I'll find you hip cats in the lobby," he says, doffing a
fedora I hadn't noticed before. When the door shuts, I stifle
a giggle.

"Wow. That was not who I was picturing, for RA
Jeff."

"What's that supposed to mean?"

I backpedal a little, having found myself on the
receiving end of Tara's withering gaze yet again. Even her
freckles can look...haughty. "Not—come on, that's not
what I was thinking. He just seemed like a jazz musician
or something. Very...sly." I pretend to hunt around the
room for shoes, well aware that Tara's eyes remain on me.
She doesn't bark out some snappy comeback, though.
Guess there's a first time for everything.

"You wanna know what I think?" Tara asks after a
moment, while polishing her Mod Squad ensemble with a
furry white stole. "You've never been in love. It's rarely
who you'd expect, you know. Wait!" I open my mouth to
protest, but Tara has suddenly fallen to her knees. She
roots around by my headboard until she locates her

treasure: that book she flung at my head the other day. The Enlightened Orgasm.

Clearing her throat dramatically, Tara opens her tome and reads aloud. Her voice is warm, coating the words. "You recognize love when you've never seen it before," she says, then appears to wait for my response. I say nothing. She looks up at me, blinks her eyes twice behind jeweled faux eyelashes, and snaps the book shut. She smiles her maniacal smile. Via a very small inclination of her head, I understand it's time to go.

Chapter Seven

* * *

RA Jeff drives us through Hillcrest in a fusty old black Bimmer, which I know is not actually expensive because there's a hole in the floor through which you can see the street go by, if you're riding in the back. I prop my feet up against the passenger's side. Better uncomfortable than dead.

"Tara tells me you're an artist, in addition to an athlete," RA Jeff says, as soon as I've maneuvered myself into a yogic position. My body stings a little, given how hard I ran today. Ugh...the pain in my hamstrings just makes me think of that moment by the tree all over again. Am I the biggest fucking idiot in the world for not letting Chase Kelly have his way with me?

"I bet you'll dig this band we're gonna see, Savannah." Right. Naturally, RA Jeff will know me by my roommate's baptism. "They're very artsy. I think the genre is 'dream pop.'" Tara extends a lazy hand in my direction, without turning to look at me. A tightly rolled joint is pressed between her fingers. Wordlessly, I take a hit. San

Diego zips past, and I lean out the backseat window to exhale and watch its transom, like a dog.

* * *

Once we're inside the crowded club, I quickly lose track of my guides. One minute, Tara and RA Jeff are pressing into a throng of bleach-blonde beautiful people; in the next, they've vanished fully into the haze. It's so hot in the Ruby Room that I find myself fanning the underarms of my cute sixties shift—you know, like a lady does. I stand on go-go boot tiptoe, scanning the sea of ultra-tanned faces the best I can. You'd think that pale, done-up Tara and her hipster companion would stick out like sore thumbs in a place like this. But...no dice.

"I know what you're thinking," someone shouts into my ear. "And you're right. This fucking neighborhood has gone to the dogs."

I swivel so hard and fast that my hair smacks the would-be assailant across the face (taking some of the "cute run-in" out of the moment), but we recover fast. He's laughing and smiling—in that arch, maddening way of his—as he picks a few strands of my blond tresses out of his mouth.

Last night's case of mistaken identities suddenly strikes me as laughable. For how could I not have known? Brendan Kelly's hair is scraggly and long in the way of someone who's relied chiefly on natural conditioners for years. He's also got the careless stubble of a guy who shaves only when it occurs to him. When someone jostles me and I'm thrown closer into his orbit, I expect to inhale patchouli oil and B.O.—but am surprised to find the air around my childhood friend un-acrid. He smells like a familiar soap, actually.

Well—soap, and the burnt vanilla of certain whiskeys I recognize.

"I like this look," Brendan is saying to me, seemingly from across some vast space. "Does Dusty Springfield know you raided her wardrobe?" I'm too busy marveling at how time can make the most remarkable shifts in a person's face to register his words at first. He looks the exact same, of course—yet totally different. His cheekbones are sharper, somehow more dominant. Or maybe it's just that he's lost the freshman fifteen he so ambitiously assumed early, in high-school. The puffy, stoner hollows below his eyes have lifted, and it appears he's actually seen some California sun.

"I like this look," Brendan says again. I watch his mouth move, registering the rumple develop between his eyebrows at being made to repeat himself. His lips, though cracked, retain a surprising fullness that his brother's haven't. It's like there's more to Brendan Kelly's face. Mysterious crannies and lines, edges alluding to wisdom and wit. He is more finely drawn than his twin.

His interesting face tilts; Brendan purses his lips. "Parlez vous Anglais?" he asks me slowly, in the garbled French from...oh right, of course. The garbled French from Monsieur Honigsberg's class, our freshman year of high-school. We sat next to one another that year, managing to distract each other so thoroughly that we nearly failed the class. I remember how we studied frantically for that final, our heads bent low over my Dad's kitchen table. No one else had been home, and during our first (of many) "study breaks," Brendan had the brilliant idea of getting me stoned. "Don't worry," he'd said, while rolling a J with a focus he never applied to our studies. "If you get too fucked up on this, we'll just drink some of your Dad's gin. Alcohol and marijuana counteract one-another."

Unsurprisingly, we'd both gotten C's in French.

"THANK YOU!" I blurt now, so loud that a few of the surfer dudes in our vicinity swivel in our direction, shoot us a San Diego approximation of the "I'm annoyed" look. Which is to say: a tense grin. That's not chill, bro.

"Somebody turn spaz in Savannah?"

"You remembered!"

Brendan cocks his head again, still not fully convinced of my sanity. I shake my own mane back and forth, as if to reset myself.

"You're not still at art school?"

For the first time, the truth feels like a confession. I'm worried Brendan will be disappointed in me, but there are no two ways around it.

"I've transferred to SDU, actually," I say, looking away. His eyes, like his brother's, are that same penetrative, algae-green. Yet Brendan's gaze is more intimidating, the way it was when we were children—but why should that be the same today? That's when it hits me. Oh my God. I almost made out with his brother. Earlier today. The memory feels strangely shameful—Chase's sweaty hands on my hips, his breath on my neck... I fight the urge to yell this odd, inopportune truth in Brendan's face. He doesn't have the kind of eyes you can keep secrets from.

"Ah," my old friend says. I search his eyes for some deeper meaning, but those green pools are inscrutable.

Then I wait for him to say he's glad to see me, or that he can't believe I'm here, but...nothing.

"I want to be closer to my Dad," I continue, defensive for some reason. "And...yeah. I've got some good buddies here," I gesture vaguely toward where I think Tara and RA Jeff have vanished, but Brendan doesn't track my hand. He won't stop staring me down.

In the ensuing silence, I allow myself to take further stock of this strange new person I used to know. He's eschewed the surfer look, in favor of a devil-may-care, rockstar in '76 attitude. Black t-shirt, ripped from wear at the collar, frayed at the bottom. Red skinny jeans, so snug they make his legs into proper stovepipes. I can't help noticing that his legs are less apparently muscular than his brother's, though their arms are comparable—thick and ropy, all sinew and bone. Only, along Brendan's right forearm, there lies a long, hand-drawn peacock feather tattoo, rendered in black and green. My heart is beating fast. It's the music, surely. Has to be.

"You were always such a wonderful artist, though." When I regain the confidence to look up into his eyes again, I'm relieved. He's smiling.

We're okay now.

It's not awkward.

"Thank you kindly," I exhale. Someone knocks my elbow again, spinning me back into the envelope of warm boy smell: soap, whiskey. Brendan doesn't flinch from (or advance toward) the proximity, so I stay close.

"I have so many questions for you," I say, still way too loud. "Like, what have you been up to for the past few years? And your music stuff! My Dad said something exciting about your band on the radio?" I will straight-up keep babbling if he does not cut me off. "I'm actually here to see a band. With some real friends. I mean, I didn't make them up, or anything. Ha."

Brendan opens his mouth to speak, and it's then that Tara and RA Jeff reappear from the ether. In the few minutes they've been gone, it seems that these two have managed to knock back some inordinate number of cocktails—or else they've smoked a great deal more marijuana. Knowing them, even as little as I do—it's probably both. RA Jeff sways side to side as he attempts to doff his fedora to Brendan.

Tara is less polite.

"Bitch, Baby's Alright goes on in like three. Where did you scamper off to?" She tilts her gaze up, shrewd eyes roving over Brendan. Before it occurs to me to intervene, a devilish, knowing expression crosses her face.

She elbows RA Jeff so hard that he goes spinning into the bar.

"My bad. We'll leave you two alone," Tara says, eyelashes fluttering. "Your costume is way better tonight, PS," she tells Brendan, who looks appropriately confused.

"Oh, Tara, no. This is actually–"

"I don't need to know, sugar. Just wear a condom." This remark so tickles RA Jeff that he fully rights himself, and seems to forget all about any probable spleen damage.

It's like every pore in my body flushes. It's like I'm having a sixth grade attack of nerves. But I force myself to look back at Brendan, affecting an expression I hope seems self-effacing and cool. He doesn't look at me, but his body shifts just slightly away from our little nest of closeness. Our little corner in space.

"Baby's Alright can't go on without their lead guitar," he tells Tara, cool as a cucumber. But is it my imagination? Is he not looking at me now? Oh my God.

Tara opens her mouth in the way of a confused, drunk person, and we all wait for her to put the pieces together. Driven by the same alien boldness that propelled me to call Chase 'handsome' on the quad earlier, I lean over and snatch the half-drunk cocktail from my roommate's clutch.

She doesn't seem to mind that I knock the fruity concoction back like a person dying of thirst.

"Oh. You're the TWIN!" she says at last, and thankfully, Brendan laughs a little. His eyes flick towards me once more, his right eyebrow cocked in that maddening, familiar way. Just the way it did in French class, or beneath the oak tree, or during any of our fervent discussions about rock n' roll. Except we're not kids anymore. We're supposed to know—and be—better.

"So I see you reconnected with my better half," Brendan murmurs, leaning in a little bit as he makes the exit gestures of someone about to leave. His greasy hair falls across his eyes.

It's a shift imperceptible to anyone but me, but something suddenly feels lost or broken. His voice has turned wry, the intensity has gone out of it. Of course, this had to happen. The Kellys are brothers. They probably talk all the time about whoever they happen to be boinking-against-trees that week. Whatever I was thinking I could get away with now strikes me as impossible folly. I've already made a choice.

"I hope to see you around, Brendan! We should hang," I shout this, too, but the younger Kelly, already paces away, just smiles at me like he hasn't heard. Tara and RA Jeff are arguing about something, in less-than-low tones. When I look to them and then back up, Brendan has vanished fully into the haze of the Ruby Room. It's almost as if he was never really here.

"He's way hotter than his brother," Tara pronounces, oblivious. RA Jeff seems to snap back to life.

"Hurry," he says, shaking off what must have been a dull interaction on his part. "We'll miss the band."

Chapter Eight

* * *

A smarter lady could have put the obvious facts together, but still: I manage to be surprised. When the lights dim in the back room. When the throng of beautiful blonde girls begin shrieking, their voices shrill and sincere. An unseen announcer plays hype man, as spotlights criss-cross the tiny stage: "Here for a very special set, boys and girls, ladies and gents of our beloved Whale's Vagina: it's Baby's Alright. You can say you knew them when!" RA Jeff has crouched to allow Tara to sit up on his shoulders, to the chagrin of all the people behind us. I don't much feel like listening to music after that bizarre scene at the bar, but I try to put on a game face anyway. I am, after all, still trying to say yes to life, in the way I never quite did in Savannah.

And what did I do wrong back there, exactly? Sure, I was excited to see Brendan. I was looking forward to talking to him. But I got to flirt with his brother this morning, after years and years of openly craving to do just that. I haven't seen either of these nuts in years—so where is this guilt-storm coming from? I don't owe either Kelly anything. Not yet, anyway.

"Tara?" I call up to my roomie, unsure of what I'm about to ask her but certain her response will be soothing. She turns her eyes to me, but just then, the stage is swallowed by a furious power-chord. The spots stutter off, then on, and suddenly—he's here again. Only this time, with a bright red electric guitar in hand.

"This one goes out to a blast from the past," Brendan Kelly grumbles, his onstage voice a shade more gravelly than his tone at the bar. It's very, very sexy. Of course he's the lead man. Of course. "Avery Lynne, San Diego's glad to see you again." He closes his eyes. He already seems shinier, more brilliant under the stage lights—a pearl of sweat hovers at his hairline. His eyes don't hunt for me in the crowds, which I kind of love. He just believes I'm there, watching.

"Why didn't you fuck this guy again?!" Tara slurs down at me, while Baby's Alright rolls into an aggressive intro. As I'm straining to hear the song Brendan's taken the trouble to dedicate to me, I wave drunky away. She's clearly still confused about which twin is which.

Brendan returns to the mic, but not before sliding a hand back and up through his glistening locks. His lush mouth falls open, and his eyes sink to the neck of the guitar. His expression is at once violent and tender. His passion is riveting to witness. Like a whinnying horse, he bucks his head and begins to sing, the tendons in his neck rippling with effort.

"Runaway, runaway—though you told us all that you would stay/ I watch your future float away/ runaway—runaway." When I lift my eyes from the stage, I see that the sea of women in the audience are singing along en masse to Brendan's words. His own gaze remains fixed on the neck of his guitar. His fingers run up and down the frets like busy insects.

"He's good," RA Jeff barks in my ear, nodding his approval. I furrow my brow. It's probably nothing, I tell myself. He dedicated his hit to me. That's all. It's sweet. Don't read into the lyrics, Lynne. Not everything is about you.

Brendan's hair is all but obscuring his face when he staggers back to the mic for a second verse: "...too afraid to do the brave thing, bright eyes/ too afraid to take the chance. And it hurts to see you wasting time on a ghost of old romance..."

When I glance up, Tara is mouthing along with the words it seems she couldn't possibly know—but then I remember. They're on the radio here, Baby's Alright. All of SDU could know this song.

The lights shift onstage, so Brendan suddenly resides in a lonesome spotlight. The song slows down, the words repeat. The bearded rhythm guitarist begins a slow clap, over his head, indicating the crowd should join. But I can't move, for fear of missing something in Brendan's comportment. The spotlight suits him—his oiled blonde hair glints, dozens of droplets of sweat now dance from the ends of his strands. His peacock tattoo ripples and bends in a muscular dance with the instrument. But mostly, I watch his face. His eyes are screwed up with effort and passion, his full lips enunciate each word to the last: "Don't you know? The mirror can't talk back..."

And I'm not imagining things when, after the final syllable of his hit song, Brendan Kelly lifts those penetrating green eyes. The same eyes I knew so well throughout our mutual childhood. He doesn't even scan the crowd, but rather, he finds me immediately, locking on me like a missile. He bores holes into my eyes, communicating something, and it's like he knows and sees everything—the pain I endured in Savannah. The way I've come back to San Diego. Everything is bare to him, down to this morning's illicit jog. It's then that I understand.

This song is mine.

Chapter Nine

* * *

I remember the last time I hung out one on one with Brendan Kelly, before our friendship completed its entropic disillusion. It was after school, on a hot day towards the beginning of junior year. I was just falling in with a new crowd of people—all girls, all snarky. Two days prior, Gary Pinter had asked me to be his homecoming date. I was taking my first studio art class, and excelling in watercolor.

Typically, I'd badgered one of my driving friends for a ride home, unless I was staying after school to paint— but on this particular Thursday, I'd waited too long to make my pleas. The sky was dark, filled with low clouds promising a rainstorm. Dad was working a late shift at the college. Just as I was packing up my heavy canvases and paint-box in preparation for a miserable trek back home on the city bus, Brendan Kelly waltzed down the hallway. Steel-toed boots clacking. (This was during his short-lived punk phase.)

We were already getting awkward with one another, by then. The gossipy rumor mill at Giuliani had plenty to say about the less-anointed Kelly: namely, that he was a burnout, and frequently got it on with a number of burnout girls I made a habit of being afraid of. On this particular day, he had all the accoutrements of an alt kid: acoustic guitar slung over one shoulder, skateboard dangling from his then-chubby wrist.

"As I live and breathe!" he'd yelled, friendly as ever, on seeing me struggle with my canvases. Brendan kicked his skateboard flat and glided along the ground in my direction. He'd shouldered my paint box with ease, even though he was already laden with crap.

"Brendan, no chance you have your brother's car today, right?" It was well-known that Chase had gotten a beat-up Nissan (dubbed "The LoveMobile") for the twins' last birthday, while Brendan had opted for a red Fender Strat.

"I have a key to it, if that's what you mean." He'd wiggled his eyebrows, I'd laughed. Moments later, we were racing under leaking rain clouds towards The LoveMobile, me struggling to protect my canvases from the imminent downpour.

Once we'd reached the car and the locks clicked shut behind us, Brendan and I had both started laughing, as if we'd just escaped a certain death. Away from the austere school light and the possibility that someone might catch us (but doing what, exactly? I didn't know), I let myself relax. I let my wet hair loll against the head-rest, I stretched my legs long. I remember the car smelled like Chase—which is to say, of tennis shoes and Axe body wash.

Brendan and I hadn't spoken. We hadn't needed to, really. I'd let my eyes flutter closed, while my old friend ministered to his then-favorite hobby of joint rolling. I'd felt the car battery thrum to life around us, and heard Brendan begin to fuss with the radio dial. I tilted my head to watch him, his shiny, wet face bent low with concentration. He didn't meet my gaze until securing an oldie, on the KISS FM station: "Wish You Were Here," by Pink Floyd.

"Oh, change it! This song is so sad!"

"It's not sad. It's melancholic. There's a difference."

"Always so pretentious, Mr. Kelly."

In lieu of response, he'd smiled in the direction of his joint, which now lay fully prepped in his lap. But he didn't light it.

Suddenly exhausted, I'd let my eyes slide shut again, letting peace surround me as the rain gained momentum outside. Brendan began to tap his fingers against the steering wheel. Curious, I'd opened one eye—just a sliver—expecting to catch him mid air guitar, or doing something else silly. But instead, what I saw surprised me. Brendan Kelly was gazing at me, his eyes soft, his mouth a demure crescent. In a face I knew so well in high-school for its constant lack of seriousness, such serenity was startling to see. He was looking at me in the way I sometimes saw people in art class look at paintings: with a kind of reverent satisfaction. His eyes drifted down my body in the same way, pausing to linger on my chest as it rose and fell, then finally, my hips, as they shifted below the seatbelt. And I'd just let him look at me. I'd felt no fear. The opposite, in fact: when I remember that afternoon, what I most recall is how safe I felt in the car, while a storm raged on outside.

In fact, I can't remember what it was that made me finally say, "Wanna start the car, doofus? I've got shit to do." But in any case, the spell was broken. I'd opened my eyes and pulled a face, then he'd pulled a face. We traded some jokes and some small talk. He'd dropped me off at my Dad's and, after waiting to see me inside my house, had pulled off without so much as a wave.

* * *

I've officially abandoned unpacking. Let the chips fall where they may. Instead, unable to sleep, I've rescued the paint box from its corner, and rustled up a small, un-stretched canvas I've permitted to languish in the bottom of a duffel bag. I don't know what I'm painting. I'm mostly just mashing colors together, an attempt at making meaning from emotion. The room is my own, as Tara's spending the night down the hall, with RA Jeff. It's just me, my paints, and the window looking out over the quad. Oh, and the tattered copy of The Enlightened Orgasm, fanned face-down on my roomie's bed.

Leaving the club, I'd been restless. The rest of Baby's Alright's set had passed in an odd blur, during which I was extra-aware of the people shifting around me. Everyone seemed to have noticed the way Brendan's lyrics had been aimed directly at me, like some kind of arrow. Other girls looked at me in my peasant dress with a look that was one part pity, one part envy. Finally, I'd insisted my trio return to the fusty black Bimmer, claiming a headache. RA Jeff had even seemed grateful to toss me the keys and collapse in the perilous backseat, while Tara slurred directions from the bucket seat.

The whole drive back, though, I'd fought the impulse to hang a U-turn and speed back to the Ruby Room. In an ideal world, I'd go up to the dressing room door and demand that Brendan explain himself. What did all that "too afraid to do the brave thing" shit even mean? And if "Runaway," was actually a hit on local radio—well, what could it have to do with me? When did he even write it? Those lyrics described a woman who didn't know what she wanted, a lost little baby. This was an assessment I resented. Brendan Kelly didn't even know me anymore, what right had he? Yet this whole malformed speech seemed at odds with the way he'd looked at me, shot me that gaze that said, "I know everything."

"You're awful quiet," Tara had said, after redirecting us out of a third wrong turn. "Is everything okay?"

"Dandy," I'd said, eluding some facts. I've been at school for all of two days, and I already feel like I'm playing Monkey in the Middle with a set of twins. Yup. Everything's perfect.

Ever the social-cue reader, Tara had clammed up after that, though I thought I could tell from the way she pursed her lips that she had opinions to share about my predicament.

If it's even a predicament. Fuck.

I debate calling Zooey, or even my Dad—but it's too late for both. Besides, I should give my best friend some space to cool down after today's little skirmish. Yet I don't quite want to be alone. I drop my brush, and let my eyes swivel towards the book on the bed, its opaque words of wisdom: You recognize love when you've never seen it before. I still don't quite get it, but I'm intrigued.

Leaning back in my narrow bed with the book propped against my chest, I begin to read. The very title of chapter one ("Your Clitoris is a Singing Bowl") nearly makes me laugh out loud, but I recall Tara's intensity. She'd basically sworn by this book. It could very possibly have something to teach me, especially given the current...state of affairs.

"A good partner knows how to press all the right buttons," I read aloud to myself. My imagination drifts in, arranging a specific image: strong, taut arms, surrounding me. A tan, tapered chest rising and falling, inches from my own. The puckered pads of callused fingertips, drawing a line from my clavicle to the pulsing place just below my belly button. Green eyes.

I read on.

"He should know your body, inside and out. He should be able to speak its language." Full lips, pressed against my ear, rasping words so low I can only discern their intent. Damp, shaggy, blonde hair, tickling my nose and chin like gadflies. I know this body. I've known this body for a long time.

I let the book collapse onto my chest as I slide a single exploratory finger below the elastic rim of my panties. My eyelids flutter shut as I press against myself. In my mind, he grows assertive. His hands press my arms up and over my head, as he clenches his thighs around me in a straddle. His manhood strains toward me from beneath snug boxer briefs, and I push against his grip to rise and bear witness to his erection. He's taut and thick and I yearn to hold him in my palm, but he won't let me. Not just yet.

Instead, he begins to kiss my neck. His lips fall lightly at first, like footsteps in snow. He moves from the hollow below my ear to the rounded curve of my shoulder. I'm aware of my softness in his arms, the smoothness of my own skin. I want to be the water he can swim through.

His hungry eyes swivel to my naked breasts, which quiver as if frightened in the spell of his glance. He moves slowly, his full lips falling on one hardened nipple, then the next. The first time, I feel his stubble scratch my flesh.

But the next kiss is a union of two smooth surfaces. The next kiss, he latches onto me, and begins to suck.

Though I'm tamped below his considerable weight, I still feel the heat building between my thighs. I'm aware of the blood swirling and boiling inside both of our skins— the two separate, craving mammals we consist of. We are animals. Accordingly, I open my mouth wide and release a guttural sound into the thicket of his blonde hair.

"Avery," he murmurs into my flesh, mouth now drifting down my naked expanse. He kisses a rib. He kisses the patch of muscle where I believe my diaphragm to be. Each time his mouth finds me, I shudder afresh, like I'm being touched for the first time. On the bed, I begin to buck against myself, finding my finger sticky with want. My forehead is damp with sweat. The urge to moan is strong, but I repress it. I restrict this little drama— enlightened or no—to my imagination.

When he finally pauses, mere centimeters from my dark triangle, he tilts his shaggy head up, so his chin rests on my pubis. He blinks, slowly, and I look into his eyes. They're the color of some jewel, some river, so many memories. "Avery," he says again, his face becoming agitated. He wants something from me.

But I can't complete the exchange. I can't say his name. I can't say his name because, for the life of me, I'm not sure which brother he is.

Chapter Ten

* * *

The round tables in the preferred dining hall on campus comfortably seat four people and five trays, which suits me, Tara, Trevor and RA Jeff just fine. I'm pleased to have collected a crew—especially one as ragtag as this one. The guys treat me like I've always been Tara's roommate, assuming I know each and every one of her insane stories.

"What about that dude from the Ukraine?" Trevor asks, through a mouthful of arugula. His make-up is still not quite all the way washed off from the party a few nights ago. Then again, perhaps this is deliberate.

"You didn't know? Gay!"

"No shit!"

"Yes, totally gay. I could have fixed the two of you up."

"No thanks, m'dear. I love you, but I am simply too well-adjusted to go trawling for sloppy seconds." Trevor swallows with finality, pushing his barely touched plate away. "He was cute though."

RA Jeff is a little less bawdy than his lady friend, preferring to divert the conversation with bureaucratic gossip. He informs me that there are a bunch of fun, PG activities also taking place during "Fuhgettaboutit," and I needn't necessarily go crazy every night with "the skeleton twins here." I wait for Tara to protest, but she doesn't—she just sips her nasty Splenda Pepper. No one mentions the night before, at the Ruby Room. Tara's so cagey, in fact, that I begin to think that the whole evening was a dream—not just the part I spent alone.

I'm finally beginning to spar and chat with the others, when my phone buzzes. Eight eyes glance towards my battered iPhone, and three people manage to exchange glances as I dive for the evidence. But it's too late. Everyone's already seen my message.

"You snoops!" I say, affecting easy laughter as my stomach drops. I begin to chew on my lip, as the text materializes. It's from Chase.

"Hey, Angry A. Had a blast trying to keep up with you yesterday. Now how's about I take you out on a proper date? :-) " Smileyface.

Smileyface. I feel like the dumb emoticon has shaken something lose in me. Chase isn't playing coy games; he's just trying to get to know me. I'm mad at Brendan, I decide in the moment. I'm mad at his presumption, and the way we lost touch. Chase and I could really be something. At least he's being up front with me, and not professing his feelings through vague-ass rock songs.

When I look up at the faces around me, each one pointed as a question mark, I allow myself to cop the emoji. Tara reads me fast.

"Got another date with the prom king?" she grins. I nod, quickly. Then I snap my phone shut, evading further questions I don't have answers to.

* * *

I puff nervously on a pilfered American Spirit, shifting from foot to foot in my espadrilles. A warm breeze eddies around my shoulders, lifting the hair from the back of my neck. I check my phone, for something to do:

8:10pm. He's officially late.

I've also officially received a dozen messages from Zooey, who can't seem to decide if she's angry or sad about my behavior on the phone the other day. I furrow my brow, but click the screen dark anyways. I can't deal with that mess right now. My mind feels like it's racing and racing around the quad, unsure of where to settle. I name the feeling, with a pang: it's anxiety.

It occurs to me that the ball of anxiety currently sitting in my stomach like a lump of undigested cheese perfectly echoes the nerves I shook off before that fateful gym class, all those years ago. I feel the way I felt in the moments before I resolved to run and catch up to Chase Kelly on the soccer field. I scrunch my fingers through my damp hair, turn my gaze in the direction of the dark sea. I am woman, I tell myself, making a mantra. Not even my OG crush can bring me to my knees. Hear me roar.

And, I mean, technically? This is still just our second date.

I see the glint in his eyes first, flickering from behind some palms a few yards down the quad. Then, some moonlight briefly illuminates a patch of his shirt collar. He's wearing a white button-down, with the first two buttons undone. The shirt's untucked, drifting over pressed khakis cuffed at the ankle. His hair is lightly gelled, swept away from his face. By the time I'm able to confirm his eyes, he's standing right in front of me. The completed Chase Kelly image is preppy-clean, the living opposite of his rock-star "brother" costume from the other day. Yet I can't help thinking that this look feels just as deliberate on him. Maybe he wears all clothes with this mannequin-like stiffness.

"You're late!" I blurt. You know, before something cooler comes out.

"I'll never catch up to you, I guess," he says, smirking. I pull a face at the dopey line, but Chase Kelly ignores it.

"You look great," he murmurs, leaning down to kiss me on the cheek. His lips are dry and smooth against my face. I lean into the contact, remembering our moment the other day, by the tree. He smells great. Perfume-y, but great.

"So where are you taking me, ole buddy ole pal?"

Chase just smiles, continuing to look me up and down. His appraisal takes so long I debate whether or not to repeat the question.

"It's a neat little Italian place, in walking distance," he says, finally. "Best chicken piccatta I've ever had."

I'm about to tell him I've been a vegetarian for years, but I bite my tongue. Maybe he'll remember, anyways. In Angry Avery fashion, I declared my PETA-lovin' authority in the seventh grade, and spent many afternoons talking the twins' ears off about animal cruelty.

We begin to walk, side by side through a jasmine-scented night. The tall windows of the school buildings are mostly dark, sentinels waiting for the influx of students who will flock to this campus in just a few short days. I already feel like I've been at SDU for weeks, but it's only really been a handful of hours—how strange, I muse, that time moves this way. Chase's eyes dart through the pitch, like he's scanning the area for any would-be predators. Or people who recognize him? No, no, I'm being neurotic.

"I'm nervous for when school starts," I say. "Fuhgeddaboutit is starting to feel like Never Never Land."

Chase moves a gentlemanly hand to the small of my back, guiding me lightly past an anthill in my path. I feel my face grow hot, and am briefly thankful for the cover of night. Though, to be honest, I might've preferred a lunch meeting. I want all my new classmates to see me on Chase's strong, safe arm.

"Oh, it's cool," Chase smiles, his eyes at my hairline. "I mean, I'm going into intra-football practice pretty soon, and those games are a lot of fun."

"I didn't know you were on the football team!"

"That's because we didn't talk much yesterday," Chase says, his voice low. He smirks. As we're moving, I brush up against his shoulder and feel a wave of jitters stripe my spine. His rounded, perfect bicep strains through the linen. Smooth and strong like the rest of him.

"But seriously, Mr. Kelly," I say, planting my feet and turning to face my date just as we've reached the campus' edge. "Can I just say that it's so nice to see an old friend here? I was sad to have lost touch with you guys. I'm really glad to be home again." Oh my God. Avery? Are these actual tears welling up in your throat, from nowhere? I swallow, hard, foisting away the unwanted emotion. The girl Chase Kelly deserves, I decide, is no crier. She's a supportive, staunch, team-player. She lets him set the pace, but she can keep up.

Chase doesn't appear to have caught the weird flicker of feelings I've accidentally let escape (another thanks to the moonlight), but I do see him smile. Genuinely. With all of his teeth. He takes my elbows in his hands and draws me forward, so I find myself level with the smooth patch of chest peeking out from beneath his shirt. I'm folded into a warm embrace.

"I'm glad to see you, too, girlie," Chase murmurs into my hair. "It's gonna be just like old times." He holds me for another long beat, and I feel his fingers begin to make circles along the exposed skin of my arms. But I pull away anyways, shaking myself. I am suddenly cold.

"Still want to go to dinner?" Chase asks, cocking his head. His eyebrows all but wiggle. "Or should we just...?"

I fake-punch him on the shoulder.

"Yes, goofy. I'm a lady, remember?"

Neither of us says anything for a moment, we merely hover in proximity.

I'm reminded of this one time, way back when—the three of us had been horsing around my Dad's house, involved in a long, elaborate game of hide-n-seek. I'd found myself in a linen closet with Chase, where we were tasked to remain completely silent while Brendan skulked the property, hunting for us. Brendan was a killer at hide-n-seek, and evading his watchful eye was like the Holy Grail of our after-school activities.

We must have been thirteen, so while the concept of "7 Minutes in Heaven" wasn't foreign, it also couldn't have been far from our minds. Chase and I had both wound up in the closet by frenzied happenstance, and I remember how close we'd been. How stiff we'd held our bodies. We were quiet enough to register the divergent rates of our breath. I remember the sensation of blood pounding in my ears.

"Come out, come out wherever you are, goddamnit!" Brendan cried, lurching through the house like a cranky old man. I'd stifled a giggle, and Chase, accomplice, had raised his palm up to my mouth. I still recalled the smell of the inside of his hand—the tang of sweat, the echo of soap, something else strange and sharp and earthy. He'd held his palm against my mouth for whole moments, and he didn't flinch away from me as we listened to Brendan rumble off down the hall, away from our secret nook. We stood there together, vibrating like plucked strings, charged and young and unsure. I told myself after that nothing would have happened, even if I'd wanted it to. We were just friends. Melora was on the scene by then.

Yet here, now, at SDU, while our feet straddle the campus threshold—I'm forced to re-evaluate. Were we ever 'just friends,' him and me? Could we ever be?

I open my mouth, though I'm not sure what there is to say. I've had a crush on you for nearly ten years, but I'm not sure what I want to do it about it now...feels wildly inappropriate. Chase's green eyes are alert and hopeful; his gaze stays fixed on my face. Him and me—we feel like more than dating, more than sex. Him and me, we have a history. And now I'm just standing dramatically in the moonlight, like some tragic subject of a Munch painting...I wish he'd say something.

Right when I think I've got the beginning of a sentence ready to go, Chase darts towards me—an animal move. His lips connect briefly with the corner of my open mouth. I'm so surprised I laugh—two short 'HAs' right in his face. He cracks a grin containing more light than the fake-ass gas lamp flickering above our heads.

"I can see you thinking," Chase says, turning. He takes my palm in his and squeezes my fingers. "Don't think so much."

Chapter Eleven

* * *

Chase Kelly eats with his whole body, in a way that makes me think of both a machine and a shark: his muscular shoulders hunch forward, his eyes become focused pinpricks, and his silverware becomes limbs. I can't help feeling a bit surprised by his estimation of the chicken piccatta at "The Cottone Brothers' Fine Italian" as "the best he's ever had," because he isn't savoring his meal at all. Some sneaky waiter could probably replace his dish with a bowl of dog food, and I'd be hard-pressed to imagine Chase noticing. But I guess that's an athlete's prerogative. His food is just for fuel.

"I was glad to see you could still keep up with me, the other day," he says, during one of his few pauses for air. I'm merely picking at the overcooked fettuccine swimming in its own sauce, on my plate. You know, just being judgmental. As I do.

"Likewise," I say evenly. Smiling sweetly, Chase sets his knife and fork down. He reaches across the linen tablecloth, lifts the bottle of sauvignon from its cooling basin, and expertly pours me a few more fingers of wine.

"You're tired of talking about running, huh?"

"No," I lie, indicating 'when' with my hand. I smile at Chase. He smiles—again—at me. At precisely the same moment, we each let out a giggle, and just like that, some odd, clinging tension drifts away.

"You know," I say, taking a brave third stab of my lukewarm dinner. "I forgot to tell you. I saw Brendan yesterday! I accidentally went to see his band play!"

Chase leans back in his chair. Over his shoulder, I watch a new couple enter the restaurant, pausing to fidget by the host stand. The Cottone brothers seem to have the monopoly on first date dinners in the outer-rim of San Diego.

"I know. He told me."

"Oh. Right."

"Part of that whole twin thing, you know?" Chase winks, and a sixth grade me melts for a moment. He leans forward, so the open lapels of his shirt stretch wide, revealing more collarbone. The fake candles glowing on our table cast elegant shadows on his blonde locks. From the corner of my eye, I register the woman by the host stand, looking our way.

I am with the most handsome man in the restaurant, I think. That has never happened before.

"So what did you think of the band?" Chase asks, his eyes swiveling back to his meal. The salad remains unperturbed on one corner of his plate, and I find myself staring at the halved cherry tomatoes, as if they must contain some clue. The memory comes flooding back anyways.

I guess I thought that if I preempted Brendan—if I put him in space first—then perhaps I'd be reclaiming some of his strange power over me. It would be so much easier to believe that nothing had passed between us at the Ruby Room. And the farther away from his eyes I got, the easier it seemed to believe the convenient narrative: the one where Brendan hadn't written a song about me. The one where Brendan hadn't looked at me with such plaintive, perfect certainty. But then, about what? What could he be so certain of, after all this time?

"Personally, I don't go in for all that artsy shit," Chase says, in a voice that's a few decibels louder than most of our conversation so far. I'm stabbing at my pasta, now. Anger has returned, despite my best efforts. "I love my brother, but it's like he thinks he's the savior of music. People just want something they can dance to."

"Oh, I think some people like to..." What, Avery? Think about their music? Experience catharsis in concert venues? Once again, I find myself unsure of how to finish the sentence. But perhaps I'm not giving Chase enough credit. He's a smart, sweet guy. And he told me not to think.

"I'm not saying their music is bad," Chase plows on, spearing a last bite of chicken and eyeing his wine glass. "It's cool that he's found his niche, or whatever. Just not my bag. You know?" Finished with his meal, Chase grins at me with an easy satisfaction. His questions are not really questions; I'm savvy enough to see that. I don't think we've ever had an argument during our whole friendship, and I can't imagine him mad at anyone. I return his pleasant gaze, keeping my eyes on his mouth. This invites memories from last night, in my lonesome dorm room. The span of his nakedness, alive in my imagination. We are still those kids, breathless in the closet together. Aren't we?

"Hey, Brainiac. You wanna get out of here?" Chase cocks his head, impish, uncomplicated. This is actually a question. I am definitely thinking too much, I know that. So instead of forming words, I simply nod.

* * *

Ever the gentlemen, Chase waves away my offer to go Dutch—though he does ask the waiter for a doggy bag for my fettuccine, claiming he'll personally make sure my leftovers don't go to waste. The night has grown cooler in the last hour, and as we walk back towards campus, I find myself wishing for a coat.

Using only the necessary words, Chase guides me the long way back. In fact, we take a similar route to our running path, from the day before. I'm beginning to connect patches of campus, creating a key for my mental map. A not-so-small part of me is beginning to wish that Fuhgettaboutit would never end, and instead of school, I could just keep living my new, fabulous, party girl life.

We reach a stretch of grassy knoll I recognize—the great big live oak we touched against, only hours before. Chase, for his part, shuffles from foot to foot. Is it possible that he—king of the frat boys—is nervous?

"I had a lot of fun tonight," he says. His smile is toothy and wide, a childish grin I can't help returning. Then, motivated by some unknown instinct, I press my cool palm into the center of his forehead. I fan my fingers through the fine, dense corn silk of his hair.

"Do you want to come up?" he asks. A real question. Gently, he pries my hand from his face, coming to grip me lightly about the wrist. His gaze is light and casual, but I'm aware of his strength. The heaviness of his arm, as he brings my hand to his side. Through the khakis, I discern the rounded knob of his hip bone. The fleshy barricades of muscle on either side.

We stand in the limbo for a moment. But Chase bridges the gap. He inclines his head like a hungry baby bird; he's expectant and silly in the same gesture. When our lips connect, I wait to feel the furnace of desire begin to churn in my stomach, the way it had only hours before (and days before that, years before that...). His lips are soft and probing. When I reach his tongue, it's firm and thirsty in the same way. His want, like his hunger, is unabashed. Inevitable.

"I'm not sure," I hear myself say. I've felt like such an alien to myself all night, and this final surprise is so infuriating that I feel a hotness build behind my eyes again. But I absolutely won't cry, here on this date with my childhood dream beau. I won't do that because I'm not totally insane.

"Chase, I should tell you," I plow on, breathing deep. His hands have wound themselves around my middle. We're so close, I'm surrounded by both of our spaghetti breath. Were it lighter out, I could probably discern the blemishes in his face. That is—if he had any. "I had a bad experience at college in Georgia. It's why I left, actually. And I'm not sure I'm ready." No sooner have the words tumbled out than I concede that they're true. My bones seem to sigh with relief. "And I'm sorry if I'm being weird, or...anyways. I had a really nice time, too, I just need to take this very slow."

In the ensuing silence, I try to predict how I'll feel when Chase Kelly peels himself away from me, face contorted in mock apology, slurring out some classic Dude excuse. I know him well enough that I trust I'll be able to detect the BS in his eyes, the lie lurking behind "of course I'll call!" Will it crush me? Having to lose him twice?

And I suppose it isn't fair, asking a dashing college sophomore if he's willing to wait for you, a nobody, for an open-ended amount of time. I shut my eyes tight and conjure his hulking body above me. This ground cedes fast to the Anger, the righteous Anger of Angry Avery. Anger directed at the boy in Georgia who thought he could ruin me. Anger at the twin brother, for thinking he could shame me for it. Anger at myself, for letting all these men get to me.

"Hey," Chase is saying, his fingers suddenly on my cheek. I only realize I've been crying when he holds up the pads of his left hand, demonstrating the dampness. And then I'm crying harder and more, because he's actually saying what you want a guy to say in this moment, and he's saying it while his green eyes stay steady on mine. "I've waited for you for years, Avery. A little longer is nothing."

Then he holds me, enveloping my body like a sunny day. I shut my eyes against his pressed, white shirt and feel at home.

Chapter Twelve

*** * * ***

It's a party in my dorm room, and the gang's all here: RA Jeff, Tara, Trevor, and two fresh strangers—a tall, skinny girl with dyed grey hair and red pleather stiletto boots, and a compact Asian guy with a half-sleeve of tattoos racing up his right arm. Hostess Tara ashes her American Spirit around our squalid room with abandon. Our home may be a disaster, but my roommate's made the time to get all-dolled-up once more. She wears a long ponytail of hair extensions, black mane skimming her butt.

"Annnnnnnd?" the lady drawls, as soon as I've set my clutch down on my desk. A nineties jam comes on the playlist, and the other people in my room begin to shout and dance. Red Hot Chili Peppers, a part of me concedes. Nice. RA Jeff and Trevor lope an inappropriate tango across the crowded floor, and the skinny girl and the tiny boy nod their heads to the beat.

"It was nice."

"'Nice?' What's that supposed to mean?"

RA Jeff dips Trevor, and I realize that both of their faces are smudged with glitter.

"What is this? Like, a 'dress-up' party?"

Tara shrugs, her eyes fixed in a way that won't allow distractions. Without glancing at the two newbies, she indicates them with a sweep of her bejeweled hand. "Mabus, Louise—this is my roommate, Savannah."

"Avery."

"You see, Georgia here has already got the hottest sex life on campus. She's the hypotenuse of a love triangle with...wait for it...twins." Tara smiles wickedly, and I deduce from the dopiness in her smile that she's wasted. Mabus and Louise nod their heads a bit faster, apparently approving of me just a little bit more than they approve of the music.

"I'm not in a love triangle, Tara. Give me a break. This isn't *As The World Turns*." I flop backwards onto my bed, just as Trevor pirouettes in my direction. His glittery face is scrunched.

"You didn't sleep with him tonight, either?"

"Nope," I sigh, reaching for a blanket. Then, to elude more of the third degree, I flutter my eyes at the ceiling. I'm a big fan of my roommate and her motley gang of weirdos, but right now, I wish there was a quieter place in which to rehash my evening. I'm exhausted. I feel like I've been up for days and days, and now I want to cocoon myself in a ball where no boys exist.

I can hear Tara murmuring to our guests, and just then I wonder—what if I had known her, before all the shit went down in Savannah? My new roommate is easily the baddest bitch I'd ever met. I'd never told anyone but a few campus authorities (and now, Chase Kelly) about what had driven me from school, from the South, from painting— but what if I'd been able to tell someone like Tara? Something tells me that everything could have been different. She might've encouraged me to be strong in a way that Zooey couldn't. Or maybe the whole thing might have been avoided.

"Guys, let's disperse," I hear Trevor say quietly.

RA Jeff protests, audibly, "But I'm an RA! I'm here to listen!"

But after a few moments, the door shuts with a click behind the little party. I hear Tara breathing raggedly, then the sounds of pots and pans, ministrations above our mini-fridge. The microwave pinging. I try to make myself small and silent.

"This simply won't do, bitch!" my roommate cries. With a sharp gesture, she yanks the blanket away from my face, and regards me with something like contempt.

"You've been here three whole days. You can't get your heart all broken already. You're pretty and cool and better than that noise." Smiling tightly, she hands me a steaming mug of microwaved green tea, and clinks my glass with her own half-drunk PBR.

We don't have to say much, which I don't mind. Tara begins the slow work of taking off her make-up, by now a comforting routine. I'm reminded of being a kid and watching my mother prepare for an evening out. The calm, close feeling of watching someone you love performing a task that gives them pleasure.

On the open laptop, the 90s playlist resolves in an old up-tempo Blink-182 song, and after a few seconds of silence, Tara rustles over and changes the station. The sweet tang of green tea floods my mouth at the same time I hear his words again, right here, in our sacred space. Brendan's band. They're playing electric instruments, but their sound is so intimate and clear, it still seems like they could be in the room with us. His hand on my shoulder, perhaps. His raging eyes buried in my skin.

If Tara realizes she's awakened some beast, she doesn't acknowledge it. Just keeps taking her make-up off. My eyes scan the room, uneasy. I note with a blush that The Enlightened Orgasm has been returned to Tara's slim book-shelf. Sheepish, I swivel my eyes towards the foot of my own bed, where I find something I've missed.

Propped up in the corner by the window, folded in on itself, is a plywood easel. Cheap. My paint box rests beneath it, looking dusty and grim as ever.

"What's that?" I ask, setting my mug down on the ground. Tara doesn't turn her head.

"Mabus had an extra one lying around. He's in the art department, too. You'll meet."

"I'm not 'in the art department.'"

"You're really starting to bug me with this damsel in distress thing," Tara says, her voice cutting, edgy. I could easily chose to pick a fight, but I decide that now is not the time for one. Instead, I hop to my feet and creep up behind my roommate, who watches her own reflection in the mirror. I wrap my arms around her taut middle, and put my chin on her shoulder. When she looks up at me, surprised, I don't speak. I just mouth the words: "Thank you."

Chapter Thirteen

* * *

I do what she says. I should know by now. Tara Rubenstein is, after all, like weather: unavoidable, and best when submitted to without protest. In the last few days of Fuhgettaboutit, I am drawn through class registration like a puppy at its owner's heels. Also during these waning days, I watched the SDU campus inflate itself with students— bleached blonde bimbos, hackey-sacking pseudo-jocks, and khaki-corporate types begin to roam the quad. I keep waiting for a remaining contingent of fashion outsiders and hipsters to make their way out of the woodwork, but as the days grew longer, it becomes more apparent that Tara has found the only five weirdoes at SDU and colonized them, like a new world.

"She doesn't want any AM's," I watched my roommate yell at a frazzled registrar. "She's got an artist's temperament. What about the Core at 12:15?" Tara bullied both our ways through registration, finally handing me a schedule the both of us could live with. Holding the piece of cardstock in my hand, I felt a little sad. We had no classes together, and shared no free time. Between daily schedule conflicts and her nightly policing of the Fashion

Merchandising Club, it looked like I wouldn't be seeing a whole lot of my roommate—and first real friend in the city—during the school year.

"Oh, you'll get over it," Tara'd said, rolling her eyes at my doe-eyed proclamation. "You have a boyfriend. You're the one who's abandoning me." She spat out the word 'boyfriend, like it was a tobacco flake on her tongue. Apparently, things weren't going so well with RA Jeff.

I'd considered her words without protest because here's the thing: the boyfriend comment was somewhat true. I've seen Chase every night this week. Thursday was mini-golf, at some place in the city that we needed to drive to—a miniature thrill, because I found I remembered the exact smell and feel of his old junk bucket LoveMobile. Friday was a B- horror movie, drinks after. Saturday we went for a run, and Sunday we went back to The Cottone Brothers' pizzeria. Each date ended about as chastely as the first two. I'm pleased that Chase is so respectful of my boundaries, but it's gotten to the point where I'm unsure which of us will break first. Every evening he's kissed me good night, with one foot on the threshold of my dorm lobby and the other in retreat, and every evening I wait for my stomach to flip. I wait for some braver version to supplant Angry Avery, someone who will tuck two fingers into the V of his shirt and tug him towards me, healed and ready to jump this hot guy's bones. Yet, still nothing. But whatever, you know? These things take time.

In the interest of recreating butterflies, I've also invited Chase to come out clubbing with Tara and the gang, but he is, apparently, "not much of a dance guy." At the same time, he's managed to skirt any mention of his own friends. In particular, my meeting them.

"Maybe he doesn't have any friends," Tara wisely pointed out. "He was alone at the Halloween party, remember? Well—except for Tatiana."

"It doesn't seem a little weird to you?" I press my roomie, slurping down some more bubble tea. Tara's made a point of taking me to her favorite San Diego food joints before classes start, and this particular Thai stand is apparently the best on our coast. It is also conveniently en route to my very first class at SDU: A Survey of Modern and Contemporary Lit, 101. "I mean, I know so many people here from high school and middle school. He doesn't have to hide me away, you know?"

"He's not hiding you away. Don't be paranoid."

"Like I can help it, bitch."

Tara snorts on a tapioca ball, and we both laugh. She claims that whenever I say 'bitch,' it sounds completely unnatural.

We arrive at the stone steps of Hampton Hall, where a queue of yelling kids mill around us, in no particular hurry. The kids at SDU, I've noticed, have an ease to their whole expression. Whereas the art students in Savannah were constantly hunched and beleaguered-looking, clawing the air for their next coffee or cigarette, the general populace here walks upright. They move like they're swimming—arms swinging and easy, the humid air seeming to buoy them through space.

"You're gonna do great, sweetheart," Tara says, in a Mom voice. (Or at least, what I think must be a Mom voice. It's been a while. I wouldn't know.)

"Thanks, Sugar Butt." We hug it out over the dregs of our bubble teas, and then I pin my eyes to my new world. No sooner has Tara begun to saunter away from me than a wave of dread crashes in my stomach. I take one step. Then two. Okay, Savannah, I murmur. You can do this.

* * *

I don't see him at first, because the enormous lecture hall is teeming with distractions: a redhead with bangles rattling up and down each arm is locked in a shoving match with a tall, skinny guy whose eyes are closed. An improbable trio of dudes futz with Magic Cards in the front row, their fingers pointing and vexing like people at poker tables. A hippie guy in a poncho does squats in the back row. Toto, we are not in Georgia anymore.

Brushing the platinum out of my eyes, I duck my head and make a beeline for the third row from the back. (Always a personal favorite. Not too close, not too far...) I try not to look at people looking at me, the men and women sizing me up. I toss my hair, for some stab at affect. God: let them like me. Please let them like me. Let me just sail pleasantly under the radar for the next three years, living my secret life with my party girl roommate by night...

"You're on my coat."

"What?"

The fantasy-killer beside me doesn't repeat himself. He just pitches forward in his stooped, collegiate desk, tugging the offending coat in his wake—sending me immediately rocking towards the ground. The fantasy-killer had his feet anchored on the floor, but I go flying.

My heavy tote sails forward, smacking the back of some guy's legs. My carefully sharpened pencils all go skittering. And worst of all, I fall to the rough carpet on my bare knees, in a position I'm positive reveals my ass to the whole world of our lecture hall. "Real women wear thongs," Tara had told me, days earlier, dispensing yet another pearl of feminine wisdom from her favorite book. If my ass could blush, it'd be doing it now. I am such an idiot.

Though being face down ass-up reminds me of many nightmares, in reality, the room doesn't break out into breathless applause—I think hippie-squat guy actually snorts, from the back. Instead, I find myself quickly folded into the same cloth I was just sitting on. Bundled like a baby.

"I'm sorry," the fantasy-killer whispers in my ear, bending low to secure my dignity—and it's then that I recognize the voice. Brendan Kelly smiles at me, his green eyes wide with hope and apology. His mouth is screwed to the side in what I hope is an attempt to make me laugh. I can't help it. As I slug him on the shoulder, I break out into guffaws.

"Annnnnnd, welcome to SDU, Avery." I manage between laughs.

"I'm so sorry!"

"How many people saw my ass, do we think?" I lift my head out of the jacket cocoon, like a sheepish turtle. But most of my classmates are not watching me. They begin to amble towards their chairs, preparing for class. Brendan's hand remains on the small of my back, as I rise to a wobbly standing.

"You have nothing to be ashamed of in that department," my old friend says. I move to punch him again, but there's something in his posture that gives me pause. Brendan's gaze is even, and his lips are slightly curled. I'm not entirely sure he's joking.

So I duck my head.

Right. We're awkward together, ever since a certain someone had to go writing a cryptic song about me. It is no longer like old times.

"I'm sorry about the show," I say, to the floor. Out of the corner of my eye, I spy our professor: a tall Asian woman, her long hair piled up in a messy bun.

"Sorry? For what?" Brendan doesn't let me off easy. His eyes appeal to my own, even as I search my useless imagination for words. Green pools, identical to his brothers'—yet so different. If irises were water, Chase is packing a pool and Brendan is packing...an ocean.

"I'm..."

But also, oh my God do I need to stop comparing these two brothers. Especially as one of them is my almost-boyfriend, and the other one is just some rock star who owes me money for life rights.

Someone clears her throat at the front of the lecture hall, and that's when the laughter I was expecting before sets in around us. When I pull my eyes from his face, I register our Professor, who's placed two hands on the square center of her desk and is bending low in our direction, looking unamused.

"Would the two lovebirds center stage please take their seats?"

I watch Brendan grow coy. He flicks his hair, pushes his bangs back behind an ear with an irritated gesture, and begins to mutter protests in the direction of our professor. I watch the little gold hoop glint in his ear and can't help smiling. He's so 1992 with this whole Kurt Cobain thing.

The professor waves us silent, and I resume my seat. She starts to speak, emphatically—she's the kind of lady who moves her hands around a lot as she talks. Around us, people begin to take furious notes. But I suddenly feel like I'm trapped in a bubble. All I can see or hear, all I can consider of the world around me, is the sound and motion of Brendan's breath in the chair beside me. At one point, he lifts a golden, peacock-sleeved arm, placing it on the median between our two tiny desks. I strain to feel the tickle of his arm-hair through my shirt. It's a silly (not to mention, impossible) task, but I'm hypnotized. A moment later, he leans on the arm, so he's pressing ever so slightly against my skin. I hold my breath, irrationally fearful that if I move too much, he'll pull away. Another moment passes, and I feel his eyes on me—like, I feel the exact second his gaze shifts. The Professor carries on below us, but my notebook is blank in front of me. Brendan's chair squeaks. He swings forward, hair falling into his eyes. I'm drawn into his soapy, vanilla smell. It's intoxicating.

"What's a matter, kid? You have the hiccups?"

Oh, right. Because I'm holding my breath like a crazy person.

Because I can't very well do anything else, I turn to him and nod my head, shrugging my shoulders in a cartoony way. Brendan smiles with half of his mouth. Then, he leans forward again, until his mouth is inches from my ear. His breath is tobacco and something spicier—cinnamon or nutmeg or cloves. The sound his parting lips make when he opens his mouth nearly ends me, and my ruse, right there.

"You know the only way to cure the hiccups?" he asks. I feel myself drifting towards his body. Driftwood caught in a current.

I shake my head so rapidly that a few blonde strands smack him on the face. Which makes Brendan laugh. Not loud, but just loud enough.

"Lovebirds!" our professor is in crouching position again, her brows furrowed over the half-moons of her glasses. "We're all adults here, people. Do I need to separate you two?"

"We're actually just old friends." I respond. I'm immediately aware of the mistake. The whole hall seems to swallow its laughter. I imagine I can feel Brendan shift a few cells away from me, distancing himself from Crazy McCrazygirl.

"I give that a month," our Professor snaps back, to everyone's thrill. I never took a class with more than thirty kids in Savannah, and now I feel like I'm in the galactic senate of snickering jerks. "Now. If we're done with Puppy Hour, I'm passing around the syllabus."

I lean back in my seat, face hot. I grip my pencil, making to take notes, but I'm already too mad. Brendan has shifted fully away from me, and it's all the fault of this stand-up comedian of the English department. I mean, the nerve of some people...

The syllabus reaches our row, and Brendan leans forward again. When I catch his profile, he doesn't seem put out by the joke—just amused. He leans across my desk to hand the remaining papers back to some designated TA, and in that moment I imagine his head stretched across my lap. I resist the urge to pat his silken locks, to run my fingers through his mane, the way his run around those guitar strings.

He doesn't right himself immediately, to my delight. Rather, his mouth hovers by my ear, like he's about to say something. I feel myself begin to beat, like one big heart. My chest. My stomach. The curve of my ass, which he saw almost all of, moments ago. I realize I know what he's going to say. I can feel the words on his tongue before they arrive in space. In my way, after all, I know his tongue really well. I know the tongue's favorite foods, favorite words, the kind of songs the tongue likes to sing. "Angry Avery," he'll start with. "Lighten up."

But Brendan hovers and hovers by my face, our mere proximity enough to shoot down any "just friends" nonsense I've floated in the room, but he never says anything. I wait and wait, upright and silent—but finally decide I can't take the pressure. When I bend towards my desk and pick up my pencil, it's like some kind of spell has been broken. Brendan shifts in his seat, just far enough away from me that I can no longer smell him. And this is enough.

"And remember, people! I want three pages on the Didion essay by Thursday. Double spaced, MLA. You know the drill!" Light seems to open up the lecture hall as students yawn and stretch, begin to gather their things—but I decide this must be an illusion. Some trick of the trees drifting around beyond the tall bay windows.

I move to collect my things slowly, hopeful on some level that Brendan will say something magic like, "Wanna get some tea?" But my old friend moves fast. He gathers his things into a canvas mini-duffel, with the efficiency of someone robbing a bank. He's already at the end of the row by the time I'm standing, his hand cocked in a vague salute. He doesn't even look me in the eye.

"Seeya around, kid," he calls, hitching the bag over his muscular shoulder. He smiles, once again with just half his mouth. He's already out the door before I can call to his back the only thing I can think of to say: "Hey, Brendan! You left your coat!"

Chapter Fourteen

* * *

I only met the twins' father once, at a Career Day, in the seventh grade. I remember Clark Kelly as a spindly man, somehow improbable beside his two golden sons. Clark, who worked in the comptroller's office, was tired-looking, with tired brown hair. He was fidgety and distant as he spoke about the "tenets of smart accounting," like an addict in need of their next fix.

I knew that he'd left their mother for a much younger woman named Gloria. Gloria worked in the comptroller's office, too. I only ever saw one picture of her, in an old yearbook we three discovered on file at the local library. As we bent over her old class picture, I decided she was pretty in a bland way— all teeth and make-up. But sandwiched in between Brendan and Chase, feeling their halted breathing on either side of me, I realized I was witnessing two completely different reactions to betrayal. This was a key moment in our friendship—a day when I realized that Brendan and Chase were very different boys.

"She's kind of a MILF," Chase laughed. I got the sense he was transforming pain into something to joke about. If he couldn't get rid of Gloria, he could secure some way to laugh at her. "It's hard to see now, but I'd have tapped it. Back in the day."

"Don't be gross," Brendan had said. His eyes were fixed lamps, serious and probing. I'd wanted to shut the yearbook and go exchange mix CDs already, but something in his gaze pinned me.

"What? You've seen her titties. They're ace."

Because he was ever-polite, Brendan's eyes had flicked over me at the word 'titties,' though I was laughing at Chase's dumb comment as I'd long ago resolved to be 'one of the boys.' I'd watched Brendan's face become pensive and strange as a third color crossed his features, one I recognized from some of our music chats by the big tree. The color was pity.

"Gloria probably didn't mean to hurt anybody," he said finally, shutting the yearbook. "Still, though. I guess I wish she'd thought about us." Then he'd half-smiled and we'd called it a day, running off to play one of our silly games. But I never forgot.

"Avery?"

He was so cute when he was little. There was this little smattering of freckles across his nose that's since blended into his tan features...

"Avery?"

"Ms. Lynne?" I blink, and recall my surroundings. This is English. This is a lecture hall. This is a nervous-looking TA, peering at me like a cat, over huge glasses.

"Huh? What?"

Something nudges me sharply from the side, and then there's Brendan, smirking for me, though his eyes are pinned to the blackboard. Professor Chen is staring at us, her mouth an arc of disappointment. Everyone in class is staring in a way that informs me I was apparently just asked a question.

"Sorry, I spaced out for a moment, Professor—could you, err—could you repeat? What you just said?"

"None of these other students 'spaced out,' Avery. I don't think it's very respectful of their time if I give you preferential treatment. Wouldn't you agree?"

My face grows hot, and when I swallow, my throat remains dry. As I open my mouth to speak, I feel a soft pressure at the center of my back: Brendan's hand. I could melt, but his gesture is a steadying one, not explicitly sexual. He touches me just enough to grant me strength. I sneak a peek at his eyes, in my periphery. The green ocean is all warmth and encouragement.

"I agree. And I apologize, everyone." The tension seems to drain from the room slightly, like a balloon releasing some of its air. Professor Chen sighs.

"See me after class, Ms. Lynne," she says. The TA shifts her cat eyes back to the board, and our big, dull lesson on Didion resumes. Brendan lifts his hand away.

"Look alive," he says to me, through gritted teeth.

Last week, I might've laughed at this remark—but the past seven days have been a confusing blur. I can't look at Brendan. I don't know how to act around him at all. Sparring with Chase was easy, as was the decision to say 'yes' to a date—but I can't even articulate to myself what I'd want from a relationship with the other Kelly. I mean, do I even want to date him? Or is all this girly emotional nonsense just the by-product of a new school and a new environment? Yet I can sense his eyes on me, those concerned green irises. His jacket is still balled up in my twin bed. Which makes me sound like a serial killer...

Christ.

When I reach Professor Chen, walking towards her with the gravity of someone on death row, she immediately begins to busy herself with papers, as if she's already resolved not to look at me.

"We're not off on the right foot, are we, Avery?" She slams a book shut.

"I'm so sorry about the distracted thing. And the thing from last week. It won't happen again."

"Let me ask you something, dear. Why are you in this class?"

Because it's a core requirement, I nearly say. But even I am smart enough to know that's not the right answer.

"Okay, never mind. How's this—what do you actually like to do? What gets your blood flowing?" Green-eyed twins with opposite personalities. Hmm. Also wrong. If this is a test, I've already failed.

"I like art," I manage, and am instantly ashamed at how casual these words sound in space. 'Like' isn't a strong enough word for the way I feel about art—not by a long shot. Art is the only way I know how to understand and experience the world—that is, aside from running, which more often helps me to abandon my mind. I think of the sloppy canvases drying right now in our dorm room. Tara's been complaining for days about the stench of Turpentine on her sheets, but brilliant, bold slashes of color have plagued my imagination ever since...well, ever since the great big nothing happened last Monday. Stripes and sounds and melodies, electric, unmitigated feelings find their only home on my canvases.

Professor Chen is reading something else in my eyes, and it's too much to assume she can see what I haven't said about my passion. When she opens her mouth again, her face is rigid with the expression now familiar from my daydreams: pity. She pities me. That bitch.

"I just want you to know," she says slowly, "that boys can sometimes be fatal distractions for strong women. College can be a wonderful time to learn about your self— and, for my part, I think it'd be a shame to see a smart girl like you spend years chasing a man's affections." I am floored. My stomach seems to flex, like a bicep. I feel acid rising on my tongue, but Professor Chen has already reached the door frame, pre-empting my defense.

"Just think about it," she says to me, smiling. "And don't forget the Melville for next week."

* * *

"What was that all about?" Brendan asks, surprising me. He's leaning against a bank of unused lockers, eyes scanning his phone absently. He's waiting for me, in the hall.

"Nothing," I mutter, still livid. Like Professor Chen knows anything.

"You sure? Because you look a bit stormy."

"Oh, what? Are you gonna call me Angry Avery now?" The words fall out of my mouth more bitter than I mean them. But when I glance up, Brendan doesn't look phased. Without saying anything, he lifts the messenger bag from my shoulder, taking my burdens as his. In a charged silence, we walk towards the blinding sunlight pouring over the steps of Hampton Hall.

As the glass doors swoosh closed behind us, Brendan flicks a pair of Aviator sunglasses onto his nose and turns to face me. I'm self-conscious, half-aware of the many students milling around us on the steps.

"Listen, Avery. I feel like there's an elephant in the room."

I hear my phone vibrate, but Brendan doesn't pass me my bag.

"I don't know what you're talking about," I say, shading my eyes. The sun is hot, but my skin feels inappropriately ablaze. Brendan's wearing a worn Rolling Stones t-shirt, so thin in places that you can see patches of his skin peeking through.

God. God, God, God.

"I don't want things to be weird. I know that you and brosef have been hanging out. But..." I strain towards him, almost rising on tiptoe. I'm in the orbit again, suddenly— the tobacco, and the hair, the muscular forearms. Those pink, pillowy lips. Those thick, serious eyebrows. I want to catalogue all of him. I want—

"Hey, baby!" For a moment, I'm thrown. The voice approaches me from behind now, and familiar forearms gather at my waist. I cringe away from the surprising contact at the same time that I register the doppelganger.

"And hey, brother!" Chase calls. He perches his head on my shoulder, tilts his smooth chin so he can kiss me on the cheek. I am literally in a sandwich of twins. In spite of myself, a little thrill runs down my body. I feel my nipples perk, below my tank.

"Hey, brother."

"You coming to the big game this weekend?"

"I dunno if I can make it, dude. Baby's got a gig." I'm aware that though Brendan is talking to his brother, his eyes stay fixed on me. Behind me, Chase's eyes plunge to my neckline, where I'm positive he must see my traitorous nipples, rising below my shirt.

"Did no one tell you, J? Rock n' roll is dead!" Chase laughs into the hollow between my neck and my shoulder bone, tickling me. Brendan takes the spar in brotherly stride, rolling his eyes before he seems to acknowledge his brother for the first time. Or, more accurately, he acknowledges the picture the two of us must make: the blonde jock and his blonder lady-prize. I watch something register in that handsome, familiar face. Then Brendan smiles crookedly, and begins to turn away from us.

"Such a comedian, this guy," he murmurs. Then, to me: "I'll get at you about the homework stuff later, huh, A?"

I'm sad to see his tall, lean back disappear into a sea of other tall, lean backs, but I remember to right my composure before Chase spins me gently around. This is not the life you chose, lady, I say to myself, like a mantra. My boyfriend's eyes are kind and uncomplicated, meeting mine. And we still haven't done anything but make out yet, isn't that funny? I wonder for a moment how Chase Kelly has been able to sate his muscle-man's appetite with chaste little kisses from the literal girl-next-door of yesteryear.

"Hey, hot tamale. I got a question for you." And from apparently nowhere, Chase produces a long-stemmed red rose with a convincing dew-drop balanced on one petal. On slightly closer inspection, the rose is plastic. But a very convincing fake, nonetheless.

"What's that, pal?"

Chase drops to one knee.

I feel a nauseous wave rise in my stomach. Some of the other students on the steps pause to laugh at the pair of us. A few phones emerge.

"What are you doing, Chase?"

"Only asking the hottest girl at SDU to be my date to homecoming!" The small crowd that's gathered around us goes off like a miniature firework—girls laugh and applaud, guys crow. I smile, half with relief. I mean, what did I even think? That he was going to propose to me, three weeks into casual dating, on the steps of the biology building?

I'm aware that time has lapsed since the question when the crowd around us begins to go quiet; only then is it clear that I've been expected to respond, this whole time. I look Chase in his beautiful eyes. He's so unflappable. I can tell that if I said no, he'd simply rise, brush the dust from his khakis, and give me a noogie or something. Or maybe that's just a memory from earlier in our friendship. Maybe I should listen to his advice from all those weeks ago, and actually, for once, attempt not to think so damn much.

"I'd love to be your date to homecoming," I say, with confidence. When he rises to embrace me—a little tightly, for my liking—the crowd hoots and hollers their approval, enveloping us with good cheer.

"See, Angry? I think we make a good team," Chase whispers into my ear, as his hands settle across my lower back. He says it just like that: all defensive, as if I've been arguing the opposite point. I smile back, though with my face jammed up against his shoulder, it's not like he can see.

Chapter Fifteen

* * *

No sooner have I gotten back to my dorm room and broken the news to Tara than an uncomfortable e-mail appears in my inbox. The sender is Professor Chen, and the subject is "Extra Assignments." My worst enemy goes on to say:

Hi, Avery—I'm a little unsatisfied with how we left things today after class. However, I'm more unsatisfied with your first assignment. Your Didion paper was rushed and sloppy, and I'm positive from both your track record and your few attempts at sentence structure that you can do a better job. If you're serious about starting my course on the right foot, you'll look into the following three attached essays. I'd like 500 words on the cross-over themes you find in the Forster, the Woolf and the Chandler pieces by Monday morning. As you write, think about what the timeline of these works tells us about the evolution of American literature. Happy reading! J. Chen.

"What's wrong?" Tara asks, reading the mood shift on my face before I so much as utter a sound.

"My bitchy English teacher just gave me extra homework," I whine, beginning to pace the room.

"So? Blow it off!"

"She's already taken me aside to 'discuss my work ethic.'" Playing the full drama queen, I sink to the floor and lift my arms toward our cruddy ceiling. "Week one at SDU. This is just perfect."

"You can't cram on Sunday?"

I briefly try to imagine a world in which I am not hungover on Sunday after going to a day-long homecoming tailgate, bar crawl and dance with a bunch of jocks, but even I'm not that good. I shake my head no. And the thing is? I do want to get off on the "right foot" at my new school. The whole idea of a "right foot" is why I transferred home in the first place.

Tara still appears mystified at my reaction, but I lurch into the hallway, dangling my red (plastic) rose, prepared to bite the bullet. He picks up on the first ring.

"Hey, sweetness!" I hear familiar yells in the background. They're sounds from the student union game room—a place I already know well, considering Chase has taken us there on two separate dates.

"Hey, Chase—so, I have some bad news." Behind me, Tara flops down on her bed, shaking her head like an old timer. Is it so unfathomable that someone would cancel on a date with Chase Kelly?

"Lay it on me."

"My English professor just sent out this crazy amount of extra homework, and I think I should spend the weekend studying."

"Laaaaaaaaaaaame!" he hoots. In the background, I hear the sound of someone winning an arcade game—little victory ping sounds seem to surround the phone.

"I know, I know. But is there any way you could forgive me for bailing on the day?" For a moment, there's silence on the other end. I furrow my brow, and look back to Tara—who merely raises her copy of The Enlightened Orgasm (which is apparently my friend's only book) so it obscures her whole face.

The silence is overpowered then by the sounds of several girl-voices—high-pitched, winsome, girly-girl voices. Someone wolf-whistles. When Chase returns to the line, I get the sense that he was holding the phone away from his ear for a moment or two—and I'm reminded of the way he talked to his mother on the phone in middle school. Joanne Kelly was a worrywart in the direct aftermath of her divorce, and though she entrusted the twins with one cell phone to share in the eighth grade,

Chase somehow obtained full custody. I have many memories of the three of us, tangled in a board game, while Chase spoke haltingly to his mother on the phone because he was concentrating on something else.

"Is it okay?" I repeat, louder this time. Chase returns almost instantly.

"Baby, of course it's okay. You do what you gotta do, I get it. Totally." Someone else wins an arcade game; someone else celebrates.

"Thanks, Chase. You're the best."

"Oh, now."

"Maybe we can still go running on Sunday, if you're not too trashed."

"Ha. Maybe. Okay, babe, look—I should let you go."

"You mean I should let you go, right? Sounds busy over there."

"Just some football guys, you know. But listen—if it's English stuff you're having trouble with, you should holler at my brother. Make him help you." Ping, zip, bang! "I mean, he used to write all my essays. Err—help with all my essays."

"The perks of being a twin, huh?"

"Whatever. I'll call him up and tell him to be your study buddy. No woman of mine needs to flail in an English class."

I don't particularly care for 'woman of mine,' but I'm more preoccupied by the possibility of being locked in a library with Brendan. One on one study time would probably be too much temptation. Well, not temptation, because nothing is going on between us at all—though I can't help but wonder what he'd been thinking of on the steps earlier, while alluding to that 'elephant in the room.' Oh, Christ. Here we go again, Avery.

Now it's me who's been silent on the line, vision swimming with abs, breath, arms, and a deliberately vague man before me. I can't believe I'm so horny these days. It never goes away.

"Yes," I say, trying to make the distracted edge in my voice as pure-sounding as humanly possible. "I'd love a study buddy." I can be friends with both the brothers, can't I? Of course I can. I'm a grown-ass woman.

Across the room, Tara laughs into her book. Two full, short, 'HAs.'

Chapter Sixteen

* * *

"Which of the three did you like best?" Brendan asks me, leaning forward in his little library chair. He's wearing wire-framed reading glasses that I've never seen before, and this little nod to hipster fashion jars with the muscle-man tank-top that's currently showing off his biceps. I tend to watch his arms moving over the books, and less the books themselves.

"Avery?" His tone is patient, but it shouldn't be. He's given me two hours of his Saturday already. I've wanted to gobble our time together, fill it with anecdotes and memories and things very unrelated to Virginia Woolf. As if some daffy old Victorian woman has any bearing on the here and now.

"Remember that time when we were fifteen? And you tried to buy a joint off Ethan Coakley just because rumor had it he sold pot?" I picture us by lockers, nervous, shifting from foot to foot as we argued over how much a dimebag was supposed to cost. This would have been just before the great split that drove us into separate friend groups.

Brendan sets his pencil down, and takes his glasses off his face, pinching them off the curve of his nose at the bridge. He turns to me with an unexpected quickness, then—he pulls a ridiculous face, blowing out his cheeks and crossing his eyes.

When I laugh, the librarian raises her turtle-like head and frowns at our little corner.

"Does it ever occur to you that you think about the past too much?"

"That's supposed to be the point of this class, right?" I say, gesturing half-heartedly at the old books in front of us. I've never gotten books. I would so much rather be reading paintings, pulling stories from lines and colors instead of stuffy words.

"I mean, about your past. Every third thing you've said to me is about some ancient history."

"It's not so ancient," I retort, hurt. "It's only been a few years."

"But you understand that we've changed since then, right?" Brendan hunches forward in his chair, and I spy the triangle of golden fuzz that begins below his throat and presumably darkens further down his chest. With a bizarre pang I remember my crazy, lusty day last week, when I dreamt I was tangled up in that particular skin, snug against that particular flesh. It's necessarily embarrassing to reconcile the real people in front of you with the ones you fantasized about in your own private mind, but in this case, the real Brendan is possibly even sexier than the Brendan of my imagination.

Though both are so wildly inappropriate, I struggle to remind myself. Yanking my gaze from his arms, I resume the conversation with effort. My body hums, because apparently just being in his presence is enough to make me excited.

"My brother, me, you—we're all very different people now."

"Why are you saying this, Brendan?" I laugh. "I can see that you're different. I mean, you're taller. And the bands you like have even weirder names." I indicate the little logo in the corner of his black tank: gothic-looking script spells out 'Unknown Mortal Orchestra.'

Brendan resumes his intense face, his crooning face, and I get the sensation that he is peering into me. I look away. It's too hard. Brendan sighs.

"I want you to know that you're free to change. Nobody expects you to be the girl you used to be."

"And just what is that supposed to mean?"

Brendan opens his pretty mouth as if to say something, but stays silent. He smiles, scratches his stubble, and lets his eyes swing back towards the open books on our table.

"I'm serious, Brendan. Why do you get to be so cryptic and strange? Ever since I came back, it's like you're trying to confuse me with everything you say. Like with that song. And that 'elephant in the room' thing. Is it really so weird I want to hold on to the past? At least I understood things back then." Ooh, I am definitely Angry Avery-ing now. The librarian has actually risen from her little stool, and is striding towards us with a highly unamused expression on her face. I jam my blonde hair behind my ears in two strokes, in a gesture I hope reads as "composed."

"I knew you, and your brother, in the past. The Brendan who smoked weed and said funny things and lent me mix tapes and rubbed my back when I cried about my Mom and told me all his weird kid secrets, like how he was afraid that he'd never leave this town, and how he hated his Dad for leaving but still worried about him sometimes... that's the Brendan I know. I just –" even the librarian has stopped in her tracks, as if she's listening to my mini-rant—"I don't know what it is you expect of me. I really don't."

I actually have the nerve to be proud of my little speech for a moment. Breathing heavy, my face hot, I have the brief flickering feeling of satisfaction. Because I've finally put all my strange, conflicting feelings into words. And oddly, I feel more like myself in that panting silence than I have at any point so far at SDU. I'm not wearing a costume, I'm not trying to impress a boy, I'm not running from anything—I'm simply saying things that feel true.

But Brendan Kelly, as usual, won't make it easy on me. He reaches a hand across the table in what at first seems to be a conciliatory gesture, but his fingers stop short just a few inches from my hand. I look at it resting there for a moment. The ridges of his knuckles. The frayed tips of his prints, where he's worn away skin from so much guitar playing. The old Diesel watch on his wrist, which is apparently so well-loved that it's strung together with mostly electrical tape. Looking at this vulnerable piece of him, lying between us, I wish he would touch me. I wish hard.

"You really don't know? What I want from you?" Brendan asks me, his voice suddenly uncanny—all sweet and gentle. The mollified librarian returns to her little corner. I look up to the other Kelly, and his oceanic eyes are surging. He really thinks I should be able to guess, whatever it is. But it's just that I'm so tired of guys expecting things of me, asking things of me, taking things from me. I almost take pleasure in the word that falls out of my mouth next, its callow ring in the quiet library:

"No."

And it's like a door has closed.

Brendan takes it in stride, shaking off our dip into serious conversation as if it never quite happened. In fact, he gallantly tries to quiz me on the themes in To the Lighthouse for another fifteen minutes before taking off his glasses again and standing, so I'm perfectly, embarrassingly, level with his square hips.

"You know, if we hurry, we could make it to the last stop on the pre-homecoming bar crawl. I bet Chase would love to see you." When he smiles at me, an urgency has been drained from his face. His smile, in fact, echoes nothing so much as a dead-on impression of his brother. Dopey, demanding nothing. Which, I guess, is what I want right now.

"I'll just grab my purse, brah," I say, attempting a joke. "You lead the way."

Chapter Seventeen

* * *

The last stop on the pre-homecoming bar crawl at SDU isn't really a bar—it's a big old club that looks like it was once an airplane hangar. I sense Brendan's discomfort beside me as we sidle up to the big red velvet rope, bypassing thirty girls in sleeves masquerading as dresses. They shout at us as Brendan bends toward the bouncer, who daps him in recognition. As we're guided past the partition with a wink and a smile, I reach forward, feeling my arm accidentally graze my companion's: "How do you know that dude? Is someone a secret club-rat?"

Brendan pulls a silly face at me again, and I bite my lip to prevent an un-ladylike guffaw from escaping. I already feel awkward enough, arriving at the club in jeans and a tank top that were definitely not Tara-approved.

"Baby's Alright played here last year," Brendan explains, deftly guiding me through the scores of screaming people. He places a light hand on the small of my back, and I try not to shiver. Everyone here is drunk, drunk, drunk. "Not a huge fan of the scene, but the people who work here are super nice."

We don't talk much as Brendan leads me through the club—I tell myself this is because the thrumming EDM prevents most conversation. But the truth is, something feels dangerously broken between us. I'm not so sure that we are friends after all, given that strange display in the library. Things feel weird, and I still can't figure out which one of us fucked things up.

"Wait," Brendan says, finally coming to a stop. "Bottle service, if I know my brother. Of-fucking-course." Lifting his shaggy blonde head to the second floor balconies surrounding the dance floor, Brendan begins to scan the little clusters of fancy people in fancy booths. It's hard to see what the "bottle service" people are up to from down here, but I catch occasional glimpses: a tuxedoed wrist. Brilliant white teeth against a pulsing black-light. A woman's tinkly laughter, like chimes sounding across a yard.

"There," Brendan points, with a certainty like twin-sense. His index finger indicates the far left corner of the balcony, where even I can see a pile of draped letterman jackets threatening to teeter off a booth's edge. Brendan turns to me, smiling. "Womb vision."

I smile at him, tightly. It feels a bit like I'm being banished as he jerks his head in my direction, indicating that I ascend the stairs. And no sooner have I left his side than a tall, lovely brunette with dark skin appears at Brendan's shoulder, placing a long, manicured hand on his naked arm. "Jackie," I hear the model-woman purr—and just like that, my guide's attentions have shifted.

Chase, I think, as I work my way towards the stairs. You're here to see Chase. You're dating Chase. You're falling for...

And lo and behold, there he is—at the top of the stairs. I recognize that white linen shirt and those Topsiders, even though everyone here is wearing something similar. His hair is slightly tousled, as it was on the night we met. I consider racing up behind him, surprising him like he did me the other afternoon on the steps of Hampton. But just when I inhale, about to launch, I see who he's with.

I recognize her long, skinny arms first: they're tan and lightly freckled, exactly the same as when we were kids. Her hair is different, though. It's not in a ponytail, and she (or her stylist mother) dyed it redder. For a crazy second, it all feels so natural, like the echo of a memory always does—and after all, they're two beautiful people with their mouths fastened together, of course it's natural. I realize I could still turn around, and pretend I haven't seen anything, and carry on as before. But then he opens his eyes.

The way Chase looks at Melora Handy is a way he's never looked at me. There's this vulnerable quality to his gaze—an unguardedness I've never seen on him, not once in our whole friendship slash relationship slash whatever. The fucking gaze gives it away. In that second before he looks up and sees me, gaping like an idiot in jeans at the club, I realize that whatever this thing was between my oldest friend and my oldest enemy never went away. It's always been there.

"Hey," I murmur when he sees me, cool as hell. But my voice comes out strangled. I already feel tears building behind my eyes. Chase's face tenses, but Melora just arches a brow at me, unrecognizing. No one says anything for another breath.

"Chase, who is she?"

"Look, Avery! I can explain!"

"Don't bother." I feel like everything will be ruined if either of these two see me cry, so I turn back towards the main floor. He starts to yell my name, but the sound is lost over the pulse of the club. Even though a part of me senses I'm behaving irrationally, suddenly nothing is less important than my escaping this place. I've made a mistake coming here. I've made a mistake coming back to San Diego at all. So, I run. I run away.

Outside the club, after I nearly hurtle into the kind bouncer, I fly out of my flip-flops—but I see a twist of bobbing blonde hair round the bend, so I leave them behind. Tonight, I'll out-run Mr. Kelly. Let him try to catch me. Let any fucking guy.

I don't know this part of the city well enough to navigate my way back to campus, but I don't dare to pull out my phone. Tears obscure my vision. All I can see is their kissing faces, moving from the locker room to the club and back. All this time. I'm so stupid.

"AVERY!" His voice is scratchy and hoarse. I dodge a grizzly old surfer type in Chinos, then a terrified-looking Latina woman pushing a baby stroller. The sidewalk begins to give way to a sandy path, and it's then that I realize how close I am to the beach. My feet are growing raw on the pavement, so without thinking, I hang a left toward the beginning of a decrepit wooden staircase. Guided by a single slice of lingering purple sunset on the horizon, I dance over potential splinters. I hear the staircase give with weight when his body appears behind mine, and so I skip over the last few planks. Finally, in tandem with a jubilant exhale, my feet find sand.

This beach is utterly empty, in either direction. A picturesque stretch of white sand extends to my left and to my right, as far as I can see. The beaches circling my neck of Georgia, framing the Atlantic, seemed to be always dirty, covered with teenage debris. Condoms. Beer bottles. But San Diego's waters have, apparently, stayed classy.

I realize I'm breathless on the beach, so I slow to a jog. My lungs, strained from the sprint, have abandoned their crying jag. I stretch my arms wide, and then turn to the ocean. I close my eyes.

"Damn, girl," a voice says, also breathless. He seems to be limping across the beach in my direction. A part of me wants to turn and keep running, but a larger part wants to laugh. Oh, the cosmic dumbness of everything! I lunge forward, putting my head between my thighs in a yogic dive. I watch his long, tan feet materialize beside mine.

"Come back," he says, putting a hand on the base of my back. And it's then that I shiver. I stand up slow, and face the man who's been chasing me.

"Brendan," I breathe.

"Avery," he says. He opens his mouth and furrows his brow, as he did hours before in the library, like he's about to say something serious. And I do feel like there are a million things to say. But there's also soundless feeling, welling in my body like colors, like weather. I arch my back into Brendan's palm and tilt my head just slightly, so I'm flush against his taut frame. His eyes search mine for a second. Then, his face suddenly hungry, he leans forward to kiss me.

I suppose cold is lapping around us, but I don't feel it. Instead, I just feel a liquid warmth, passing through every cell. Brendan is eager. I can already feel his cock stiffening in his jeans. But for a second, I'm content to just be smashed against him, on this beautiful, lonesome beach. When I flutter my eyes, it's in part to check that he's here, that this is really happening. His stubble nuzzles my bare skin.

"Oh my God," I breathe, millimeters away from his lush lips. They're full and smooth, nowhere near as rugged as they appear in his rock star face, from a stage-distance away. I'd half-expected him to taste like wood and tobacco, the manly things he smells like—but there's some sweet undercurrent to his breath tonight. A sweet mint. His mouth searches mine for long, deliberate stretches. His kisses are fervent, but tentative at the same time.

"It was you," he breathes, returning to my mouth with a stronger, more ardent gesture between each phrase: "It's always been you. Duh."

"Goddamn musicians."

Brendan laughs, and I grab the back of his head, drawing him further into me. Taking my aggression on cue, he plants his rough hands on my bare shoulders, beginning to knead my arms, the muscles of my back. Against my intention, one of my thin spaghetti straps falls down. I feel exposed. I like it.

"Brendan..." I say into his teeth, drawing us back so he supports most of my head in his palm. He takes a step closer to me, and I can feel his breathing body, muscles contorting between us. I suddenly realize that he's much more ripped than I've been taking him for. There's no softness at all in his chest—he's all ropy sinew and strength.

"Brendan, I should tell you..." Then, I feel his hips push up against mine. His erection, trapped, strains against the fabric of his jeans, and I'm briefly puzzled by the size and girth I surmise. He's. So. Hard.

"What?" He pulls away for a second, and I find myself hungry again. The last glimmer of sun peels below the horizon, and the green in Brendan's eyes seems to fade. There are so many shouldn'ts and oughtas. But I can't seem to remember any of them right now.

He eases me back, gently onto the sand—like he's laying a bride out atop a marital bed. He hovers over me for a moment, coming down to rest beside me. Every movement is a check-in, but I urge him on. This body, this event, has nothing in common with my tormentor in Georgia. This is about electricity.

Early moonlight drifts through his hair, finding my face through his reading glasses. Brendan smirks, and pulls these off. He sits upright and draws his shirt up over his head, producing a cut, angular figure. I place a palm against his pecs, let my fingers run further down, so they frame his six pack. It's cool on the beach, but the space between my legs is hot. I instinctively buck upward with my hips and become aware of the moisture building between my legs. Brendan grins at me, approving. Then he puts his hand on top of mine and presses us further down his body, toward the mass in his jeans.

"Oh my God," I breathe again, before I can censor myself. Now the look in his eyes is changing, shifting from sweet trepidation back to the angsty, intent gaze from the Ruby Room the evening he'd dedicated that song to me. He knows me. He knows, most importantly, that I want him.

We both fumble with the zipper, nervous—but I'm too aroused to halt what's going to happen next. Brendan gently eases his jeans and boxers over the crest of his hips, and rises to his knees above me. His cock, erect, long and thick, flops against his belly where it's nestled in a thicket of fuzz. I lunge forward. With one hand, I press against the gap created in my own jeans. With the other, I encircle his massive member, which more than lives up to its status in my daydreams. When I bring myself fully upwards, ducking my head to wrap eager lips around him, he cries out.

"Shhh!" I whisper, giggling, but Brendan just bellows again. I suppose the beach is empty. He puts one hand on the back of my head, lightly, but I need no encouragement. Opening my mouth wide, I swallow him down.

I've never exactly loved doing this before—but taking Brendan in my throat actually makes me wetter. When I peek up at his face, fixed in concentration below those perfect blonde waves, I find myself wanting to give him pleasure. I press against myself, locating my clit through the fabric of my pants. He rocks himself against the back of my throat, groaning. After another moment, one hand buried in my hair, Brendan takes two fingers and finds my lower body, where we both press against my wetness. At his pressure, it's my turn to cry out.

Despite his distraction, Brendan's hands shake as he finds the button and zip of my Levi's. His hands are surprisingly warm as they skate across my thatch, before coming to graze my wet clit.

"God," he says, when he finds my entrance. "You're so wet." He grows harder in my mouth. My swallows become desperate. Our pleasures feed one another.

When Brendan slips a finger inside me, my eyes roll backward— so far that for a second I see the dunes rising up behind us. I lift my chest, and he draws the hand caressing my head around my neck, his every gesture like silk. His fingers fan out across my breasts, digits splaying and exploring the expanse of me over the thin tank top. We suddenly can't seem to get naked fast enough, yet I don't want any of this to end.

"I wanted you. All along, it was you," I murmur, my throat dry, the words themselves sounding parched. Smiling, Brendan bends down, so our eyes are right up next to one another. I could be swimming in those green oceans. I smile back, and he kisses me, hard, bringing his callused hand up to cup my chin towards his. Meanwhile, he presses fingers deeper inside me, moving his wrist in little circles. I open for him like a flower.

The break of the waves sounds closer and closer to the tips of our sandy toes, but this only serves to make our love feel more like a race. I sit up quickly, pulling the tank top over my head, letting my short blonde hair shake out along my neck. My nipples rise and stiffen instantly in the cool air, and Brendan makes a face like he's just found a baby bird abandoned on the sidewalk as he goes to me, hungry, fastening himself around one of my tits, then the other. His sucks are long and deep, drawing much of me into his mouth at a time. I've always found my full chest to be a heavy nuisance—enemy to my running aspirations— but watching Brendan caress me, thrilled, sends a jolt of pride through me. I bring my palms up, away from his crotch. I press him into my chest, fluttering my fingers through the hair at the back of his neck. I begin to knead the smooth, strong muscles of his shoulders, which flex against my touch. That's when he mounts me. He draws dripping fingers away from my pussy, and encircles my ribcage with his thighs.

"I want you. Right here. Right now. Just like this," Brendan says, his voice low and husky. Of course I can't refuse him. He drags his hands across the length of me, applying a pressure just shy of pain. Where his naked cock rubs against my opened pants, I can now feel actual heat. I redirect my attention to his pulsing member, return my hands to him. He's slick with my spit, and I know I'm ready.

When he rises on his knees to help me wiggle fully out of my pants and thong (giggling slightly at the awkwardness), I'm faced with his package once more. I draw him into my mouth like a hungry animal one more time, just as the sea breeze finds the crevices of my naked pussy. My bare legs tingle in the sand, my heels find purchase in the silt. With a look of focused determination in his eyes, Brendan flicks his blonde hair out of his face, grips my hips with both hands, and lowers himself down onto me. Slowly, his eyes closing again, he pushes inside.

I'm so wet that it's easy. There's almost no friction at all. A ragged, unfamiliar sound falls out of my lungs when he reaches the top of me, being plunged to the hilt. Brendan's eyes snap open at the same time, and I'm briefly embarrassed by the noise. It's just that it feels so good. So round, so smooth, so much better than any other time...I lift up from the center of my shoulder-blades, breasts swinging out to the sides of me.

"Yes," I whisper. My head digs into the sand. I move trembling hands to the taut curves of Brendan's ass, look into his face as he prepares to thrust again. The look he shoots me then is as naked as we are, as unabashed, as grand.

When he pushes in again, it's harder. I didn't think it could have been deeper, but I feel him nearly by my belly button. He grunts above me, pecs engaging: "You like that, huh? You like when I push deep into your pussy like that?" I can barely nod. My rolling eyes find the dunes again. I dig my nails into his ass, grit my teeth, and bring him forward again.

Brendan quickens his pace, pushing in and out of me faster and faster and faster now. I feel myself begin to pulse and clench around his thickness, which surprises me—it usually takes eons for my body to react this way. But there's just something about the way he drives into me; I have all of his focus, so fully. I widen my legs, to ease his passage, already feeling the damp patch we've made in the sand. My thighs are sticky with both of us, and salt from the sea air. I moan. I feel something deep inside me find release.

"I want you on top now," Brendan says, just at the top of a particularly deep thrust. Without quite waiting for a reply, he cocoons me in his muscular arms and rolls us over, so fast I can only laugh. I shake my hair out behind me. It's becoming dark around us. Adjusting myself across his slim hips, I find a new ceiling of pleasure, rocking back and forth against Brendan's erection as he hovers inside of me. The tip of his penis bumps right against my G-spot. My mouth falls open, slack-jawed. I feel myself produce an improbable dampness; I am wetter, I realize, than I have ever been.

My fingers rake his chest. He presses into my ass, harder, faster, until we're humping like rabbits. He cries out. I cry out, rocking fast, launching my head backward, so I can see the ocean. Brendan brings a shaking hand around and presses his hard thumb against my exposed clit, beginning to rub me in little circles. All of my muscles tense. My pussy contracts.

"Fucccccccccck," I growl, feeling as if flood-gates have released inside me. I come for seconds and seconds, like the ocean, lapping—he drives into me, hands roving across my breasts, pinching a nipple, rubbing my spot…his movements remind me of my daydreams, but somehow transcend them. I come with my whole body, feeling joined to Brendan. With a final spasm and shudder,

I'm aware of the cold again. The breeze gathers force. The sweat running down my body has become cool and dry.

Brendan smiles beneath me, beginning to caress my skin. I fall forward, nestling myself against the rigid structure of his chest, pressing my cheek flush against his fuzzy pecs. He puts a hand in my hair.

"Was that good, baby?"

"Ha. Ha," I manage to breathe, my voice coming out as a croak. I'm suddenly super sleepy.

"I'll take that as a yes."

We're silent for another few long beats, during which I can hear his heart, flush against mine. The two beats are a little bit off—his is faster—but I find something pleasing in the rhythm we make. It's musical, how we dance with one another. I snuggle a little closer to him.

"I want you to come," I say, half-hearted. To be honest, Mama needs a few more winks before she can ride this roller-coaster again.

"Later," Brendan says evenly, fingers finding my scalp. His touch feels great, even outside of sex. "Don't worry."

And for some reason, this makes us laugh like hyenas.

Something scuttles and drifts in the sand not far from us, catching the first strands of proper moonlight over the bay. I shiver. While still holding me tight, Brendan eases himself out of me. His erection has abated only slightly, I notice—and I'm sorry to feel him leave my body. Later, indeed.

"This was a bucket list-er," he murmurs, tickling my ear.

"Which part? Doing it with your oldest lady friend, or doing it on the beach?"

"Oh, the beach. Definitely."

"Dick," I say, mustering the energy to punch Brendan on the shoulder. Above us, I sense street lights snapping on along the boardwalk. It's time to come back to reality.

I sit up, reluctant, and roll off his coiled torso to put on my clothes. Everything is damp and dewy from the sea breeze, or from us. Brendan doesn't budge an inch, preferring to fold his hands behind his head and look smug as he stares up at the moon. His body, I must admit, is built for twilight. His glistening skin seems to rise toward the night sky with each inhale. He seems peaceful, cut from stone, and is beautifully unashamed.

"Damnit," I say, halfway into my tank-top. "Now I want you again."

"There'll be time for that," he says, finally rolling up into sitting. He reaches for my hand, and I succumb. I bend to kiss him, and he draws me in once more, mouth opening easily, tongue probing gently.

"I should..." God. I don't even know. The slurry of questions I need to answer is creeping into my mind along with the street lamps, and the sound of SDU students beginning their evening ransack of the city. I wonder what Tara and the gang are up to. I wonder—

"When can I see you again?"

His eyes are earnest orbs. All I want to do is stay on this beach with Brendan Kelly. I want to wake up here. I want the tide to carry us out, and then in again. But I also need time to think.

"Class," I say quickly, pulling away from his arms, his perfect kiss. For an instant, I catch my own impression in his eyes—glowing skin, crazy hair, raw-looking mouth. What comes to mind then nearly makes me guffaw all over again. I'll be your mirror. That silly song from a sixth grade mix tape. After all this time.

I turn to go, leaving Brendan doubled over in mock pain on the beach. I saunter in the direction of what I hope is my dorm room. I don't move fast, because I have nowhere left to run.

Chapter Eighteen

* * *

"Okay," Tara says slowly, her eyes narrowed in concern. "While I'm digging the loft aspect you've brought to our communal living space, I wonder if we can move some of these canvases." My roommate is gingerly holding one corner of a half-rendered sketch. I knew this day was coming, but as I open my mouth to apologize, my roomie's expression switches gears.

"You. Little. SLUT."

"Excuse me?!"

"Don't lie to me, Savannah. Somebody's been getting freaky. You can always tell." Tara drops my coiled paper and about-faces in the direction of her bookshelf. There, she produces her well-worn copy of The Enlightened Orgasm, and cracks open a page like she's about to read aloud.

"Tara, I'm actually not in the mood right now," I say, though my words sound to me like they're being spoken in a dream. I go to the window, press a cool palm against the glass. I said I had all these things to think over, but for once—the slurry of questions just isn't coming. Everything on the beach with Brendan had felt so right. All I can care about now is how I might go about replicating that feeling, as soon as possible.

"Is Chase as big as he looks?" Tara asks, hopping onto her bed like a crazy elf. She's wearing cheer shorts, the likes of which I haven't seen since the movie Bring It On. "And damn, that boy has shoulders on him. Did he show you the business?"

"Tara! Cut it out, okay?"

Because she's too bad-ass to ever show offense, Tara merely sets her chin and places two palms in front of her face in a mock "don't hit me," gesture. But I can see she's smirking. And she can see I'm smirking. Plus, I probably smell like beach sex.

Mmmmm.

There's an aggressive pounding on the door just then—five rapid knocks in succession. The noise jolts me. I look to Tara, panicked, but she just shrugs.

"RA Jeff?" I mouth, cocking my head. I mean, I know they've been fighting. Though to his credit, RA Jeff doesn't really seem like the 'door-pounding' type. Either way, Tara shakes her head.

"Avery?" The voice behind the door sounds plaintive and pained, and I hear it followed by five more angry knocks, strong enough to rattle the heavy door in its frame. "Avery, please open up. I need to talk to you."

My heart seizes in its cage. I take a mental stock of my body—sticky thighs, sandy legs. Tara just looks at me, her face scrunched with confusion. Then she tilts her head. Looks from the door back to me. Her eyes widen, and her jaw drops.

"AVERY!" she mouths, reminding me briefly of the mother I haven't seen in years and years.

"WHAT?" I retort silently, as I frantically cast around my crowded desk space for a rubber band. Maybe if my hair is up. Maybe if...

"You know I can hear you moving around in there!" he shouts, banging once again. "Avery, seriously! I won't go away till you talk to me!"

Tara all but pushes me in the direction of the front door. It's like she's forcing me to respond to a pushy prospective prom date. It's here that I begin to feel low.

When I open the door, the first thing that's clear is that Chase is still a little buzzed, which makes sense. But the second thing is that he went into the city and purchased make-up flowers—a dozen pink, real, roses—expressly for me. Thrusting the bouquet into my hands like he's tired of holding it, my old friend leans against the side of the doorframe, his eyes beseeching. Wary, I just look him up and down.

"Well?"

"I'm so sorry," Chase says. "She's just an old friend..."

"Yeah, Chase. I remember Melora. I remember exactly how friendly you two used to be."

"Listen." Chase screws up his eyes in a way that crinkles his handsome face, and for a second, I concede compassion. He looks sweet like this, when he's apologizing. "The thing is. We'd never said we were exclusive."

"Oh my GOD. Is that the best you can do?"

"...and you said you weren't coming out! And we haven't even done anything yet, Avery! I'm a guy, what do you expect?"

I feel myself filling up with that Angry-Avery fury— even though a tiny part of me knows he's not insane for saying these things. I mean, we hadn't promised each other anything yet. Dating is governed by the unspoken code: all bets are off until someone says they're serious.

"What do you think I expect, Chase?" I still manage to ask, my righteous tone surprising me. "We've been hanging out every night! We've known each other for years! Some common decency and respect, maybe?"

"We are dating. This is what dating is." Now smiling a little roguishly, Chase takes a step towards me. I put the bouquet between us, like some kind of barrier.

"For you, maybe."

"But weren't we having fun?"

I think back to all our cute, chaste dates—and further back, to the electric moments by the big tree after we went jogging that first day. Or the rate of my heart as we ran laps around the soccer pitch, innocent as children. We had actually been children, together. And I can't quite separate the timeline of my feelings. When, exactly, did I love Chase? And when did I stop, if I stopped?

"Listen, Chase. I like you, but..." But I don't know if we really click, at the end of the day. But I don't know if I'm chasing a ghost of something long gone. But I definitely just had my world rocked by your twin brother on a silent beach as the sun was setting. Out of the corner of my eye, I sneak a peek at Tara, whose arms are crossed. She shakes her head in awe. If even my Catwoman, power-to-the-vagina roommate is judging me right now, then I know I've done something wrong.

"Don't say anything right now," Chase slurs, his voice taking on a quiet, faintly desperate quality. He nods his head in the direction of the flowers. "Just think about it, okay? I think we make a good team. And hey, it's a pretty great story, right? 'Childhood best friends fall in love, years later?'" I grip the flowers to my chest. Chase lifts his meaty arms from the doorframe, and begins to back away. He murmurs over his sculpted shoulder, just before I shut the door:

"She didn't mean anything then, and she doesn't mean anything now. Avery. Please." His shallow eyes are soft, his manner mild. I try to remember the look he gave Melora in the club, the look I was so sure contained all the love he'd never feel for me—but I can't remember it exactly right. The weight of my recent passion settles over my skin like fine dust. Who am I to judge? I'm the asshole. What kind of girl sleeps with her supposed boyfriend's twin brother, just because she's angry with him for merely kissing a girl? For isn't that really what happened?

"Chase!" I hear myself calling down the hallway, just as my thumb slides up against a thorn on the stems in my hand. The prick feels fair. "I'll...let's think about it. Okay?"

He smiles. I smile. Tara waves her hands in the air behind me, like a deranged, human Cathy cartoon.

I. Am. (In.) Such. Shit.

Chapter Nineteen

* * *

To track down Brendan Kelly, I have to eat some more crow. I pound on RA Jeff's door, from behind which I can hear vocal indie rock of the 90s persuasion. When he opens the latch, I find my roommate's fuckbuddy in a red velour bathrobe, holding a brandy snifter. It takes some surprisingly strong will not to laugh in my new friend's face.

"RA Jeff, I need to look up a room number. It's an emergency."

"I can't just go giving out room numbers, willy-nilly. We RAs follow a code."

I can hear Tara, padding down the hall behind me in her soft bunny slippers. She's got one hand in a bag of Cooler Ranch Doritos. With a shock, I realize this is the first time I've ever seen my roommate eat an actual human snack.

"Honey," she simpers—in a voice I barely recognize—"Avery needs to look up the hot rocker guy from the other week. It's a matter of life or death." I wonder then what their recent fights have been about. I've been so focused on my own boy problems that I haven't been checking in with my roommate, like a good friend should.

As he laughs, some of RA Jeff's robe falls open, revealing a taut, smooth stomach and a few pleasing coils of chest hair. He reaches up and scratches the back of his neck, continuing to stare at Tara. It's then that I see it. For the first time. A strange line of electricity, running from his eyes to hers. For all her talk and his pomp, they're in love with each other—you can totally tell. And yet they seem so mismatched, so strange! A line from that stupid book comes to mind: you know love when you've never seen it before.

"Please," I repeat, my voice catching. It all comes down to looks, doesn't it? The Melora and Chase look. The way I feel when Brendan looks at me. "Please, Jeff. I really need to talk to Brendan. It is important."

I know that he's conceding because of the girl behind me, but I'm still thrilled when he retreats into his dorm room and returns a few minutes later with an index card.

"Use this wisely," he tells me.

"I will." I turn to go, brushing some more stray sand off my rear. I want to avoid Tara's judgmental gaze, but she plants her tiny self square in my path.

"Avery," she says, halting me with her tone. This is also probably the first time she's used my real name. A day for firsts. "Women do a lot of dumb shit just because they don't want to hurt a man's feelings. But the heart wants what it wants, okay? You can be polite and no one's slave."

Before I can respond, my roomie rises up and kisses me on the cheek. Her lips are soft and slightly sticky with gloss and chip crumbs. The gravitas almost makes me laugh again, but I know this shit is serious, so I nod instead. I admit it: there are things I can learn from my friends.

* * *

Outside, a light drizzle has begun to fall. It soaks through my t-shirt, and seems to remove some of the sand and salt on my skin. The traces of Brendan.

I take the stairs to Monroe Hall two and three and four at a time, confidence building with each step. I remember how good he made me feel on the beach, merely hours before. How peaceful, how free from the prison of my own brain. As soon as I see his face, I tell myself, I'll know what to do about Chase. Maybe we can even approach him together. That image delights: Brendan and me, holding hands on the sunny steps of Hampton Hall. Somehow, in my fantasy, everyone would turn out as friends in the end. My reconciliation with the injured Kelly would lead to a recreation of all our afternoons together under the old oak tree...just with more hot sex between two of us.

Outside his room, I can hear strands of familiar music. I haven't heard it many times, but the song already feels ingrained, somehow: Runaway, runaway—though you told us all that you would stay/ I watch your future float away/ runaway—runaway. I press my ear to the door, just to listen to my song for a minute more. It's me! I want to shout to the concrete walls of the silent dorm. I'm the runaway! But I'm back! He sang me home.

That's when I hear a woman's voice, speaking in dull tones over the music. "Brendan, it's not that...murmurmurmur...what people DO...murmurmurmur...this is what relationships ARE." I'm so shocked that I actually make a little involuntarily throat sound. In the same beat, the song fades out, and sleuth-like footsteps approach the door. When it jerks open, my face falls forward—square into the considerable cleavage of a tall, pretty brunette with dark skin who looks familiar, though I can't place her immediately.

"Who the hell are you?" the girl says, putting her tanned arms out in front of her as if to fend me off. I frantically scan the room for Brendan, and find him lying down in a twin bed, eyes glazed. He's shirtless, and idly strumming an acoustic guitar. His taped-together watch catches light from his desk-lamp. Despite the serious-sounding conversation I've just overheard, it's evident on his face that he's not all the way in the room.

"I'm Avery," I manage, eyes still roving furiously. The dorm is neat, for a boy's—neater than mine, anyways. Brendan has two or three guitar cases stacked around and on his desk, and I spy a stack of sheet music resting next to a full ashtray on his nightstand. But then there's also a bra. Long and satin and fuchsia, a fuck-me bra, draped over a post of his twin bed. Brendan sees me see the evidence. He sits up.

"Avery," he says, and his voice is infuriating. It's that famous, "Be calm, crazy lady," voice that boys are always using to subdue their ladies in public. It reminds me of...Savannah. I can't believe what a fucking idiot I am. Not hours ago, I'd let this man inside of me.

"No. Never mind," I stutter, looking from the brunette to Brendan and back again. She's putting two and two together at the same moment I am, I can see the wheels spinning in her pretty brown eyes. She purses her lips. Brendan tosses his guitar aside and takes two giant leaps towards the door.

"Wait. Please, Avery. Wait," he says to me, coming to stand beside her. They look like the American Gothic painting, suddenly—a tall, joyless duo, designed for one other. A love I've never seen, and never want to know. I turn and run, my borrowed-from-Tara flip-flops slapping wetly against the tile.

And this time—big fucking surprise—no one chases me.

Chapter Twenty

* * *

"Everyone raise a glass!" Trevor slurs, "To...well, fuck me. What should we toast to?"

"To friendship!"

"To rock n' roll!"

"Overruled," Tara crows. "Sappy."

"To not fucking needing a penis to complete you!" I holler, right in Mabus' ear. The tiny guy peels away from me, unamused—but everyone else laughs and clinks their glasses.

"Damn straight," Louise adds. "I'm all about the vajayjay lately. As an appendage, a penis is just a big, blunt rod. It lacks imagination."

"Okay, L Word," Trevor snaps, smacking his glossy lips. Tonight he wears a face of make-up reminiscent of the Glinda look, from weeks ago—glittery eyeliner, high red spots on his cheeks. Some days I truly miss Fuhgettaboutit. "Some of us have no choice. For me, man-meat is the only thing on the menu. And darlings, I do not complain."

"But men are such scum!"

"Personality-wise, often enough. But who here wants to live in a world where we can't at least Google pictures of Idris Elba's arms, and imagine what lies beneath? Or fantasize about the ass of a young Brad Pitt? The eyebrows of an old George Clooney? Face it, ladies. We are all of us slaves to the Adonis, the quarterback, the cock. Boys are our art. Penises are our pursuit."

"And white wine is not your drink."

We burst into giggles. Tara slops some of the contents of her champagne flute across the floor. The Ruby Room bartender frowns at our little band of freaks, but I couldn't personally care less. Today I turn twenty-one, and I'm turning up with my new best friends at college. I'm in a slutty dress and I'm probably failing English, but who the hell cares? Tonight, we are young. Kelly, Schmelly.

"And Tara Maureen Rubenstein, if you mention any passage from The Enlightened Orgasm right now, with God as my witness I will mushroom stamp your face." Tara pouts at this, apparently found out. Then, my roomie signals the barkeep for another round of shots.

It's been more than a week since I've spoken to either Kelly, which feels like just what the doctor ordered. In Professor Chen's class, I made a point to arrive late, when the only available seats in the lecture hall were ones in the front row. This didn't earn me any favors with the Prof (who was even less amused when she learned I hadn't completed my extracurricular assignment), but it felt worth it. The idea of sitting next to Brendan, interpreting silence and accidental brushes and coughs for an hour and a half, seemed like sheer torture.

The other brother, to his credit, has been drowning me with text messages. I received ten "I'm sorry!"s, four "Can we talk?"s and three cutesy jokes attempting to change the subject. I'd spied Melora Handy sailing around campus in the meantime, looking like a bombshell in Liz Taylor glasses and printed sundresses. On the other hand, I hadn't spied the brunette KO from Brendan's room, the girl I'd later realized I recognized from the club crawl. She'd been the one to come up to Brendan and touch his elbow, just as I was being directed toward Chase like bait. This memory, when it came to me, was only more infuriating fuel for the fire of confusion going on in my brain. I felt like I should have seen, or known, or assumed...something.

So, per Tara's advice, I'd laid low. I'd responded to Chase (with a curt but sincere, "I'm not ready to talk just yet") and avoided our date haunts, just because it didn't seem impossible that I'd run into one of the sex-addict twins out with some other girl entirely. I was determined to purge myself of the Kellys, in an attempt to locate how I really felt about both of them. You should remember that you didn't talk about exclusivity with Chase or Brendan, my ever-so-supportive roomie kept reminding me. Her maddening voice of reason act was so much harder to swallow because it was, finally, true. Neither Kelly had exactly betrayed me, or strung me along. For some reason, it just seemed easier to believe that the twins were dirt bags, who'd each taken advantage of our history, and my ever-present distrust of men.

In any case. I didn't frickin' know, and still don't.

"Stop," Trevor says suddenly, reaching across the bar and pinching me on the nose. "I can tell you're thinking about them. Stop thinking about them."

"It's not quite that easy."

"If only because we don't want to listen to you whine anymore," Mabus mutters darkly. Though we're all supposed to be some sort of posse now, I'm pretty sure this new dude doesn't like me.

The door to the Ruby back-room opens and a leggy blonde and her surfer companion swish by, trailing with them the sound of a familiar tune, being played... live. Now it's my turn to frown.

"Guys," I ask my laughing companions. "As much as I appreciate being abducted and taken to a bar on my birthday, is there any particular reason we chose this bar?"

Louise looks at the ground. Mabus smiles, a little evilly. Trevor cocks his head like an innocent doll and Tara shoots me the tight, slightly fake grin she was wearing the day I met her. What a pack of fucking charlatans. I am the worst picker of people.

"Great. Well. Thanks, and bye!" I peel myself off the vinyl stool with a little bit of effort, my ass having gotten stuck to the material. There's just no way I can face him. Not tonight. And certainly not in this slip of a dress that my sneaky-ass best friend insisted I wear.

"What if you just talked to him?" Tara is saying, as I gather my things. "Baby's Alright will be finished in a few minutes. Avery, you're totally obsessed with this guy!"

"Am not!"

"I've seen every one of your paintings, bitch! Don't lie to me!"

"I resent that! I'm an abstract artist!"

"Yeah, abstract my ass. You think I can't recognize the shape of a haircut? Or a trademark tattoo?"

I grip my drink, grouchily. The Ruby Room, so pleasant just seconds ago, now feels stifling and close.

Someone else opens the door to the back room, and that does it. My stomach shifts, and this time I can name the attendant feeling immediately: it's fear.

As I stomp away from my friends, I hear his rattling coda in my head—runaway, runaway. So, I'm a runaway. So be it.

Chapter Twenty-One

* * *

No sooner have I holed myself back up in the silent dorm room than my phone goes off. The contact photo is goofy, because I snapped her candid one morning as she was waking up—her eyes are crossed and her hair is messy. I laugh at the picture and with a pang of compassion, realize how much I've been missing the caller. Zooey.

"Hey," I say first, with no little trepidation. I have no right to expect that my old Georgia buddy would ever want to talk to me again, given how much I've been ignoring her since fleeing West.

"You remembered!"

"Of course I remembered, silly. Also, so did Facebook." I think I can make out the faint sounds of a party in her background—or at least voices and music competing for attention. She's out, and yet she remembered to call me. I'm touched.

"Listen, Zo. I'm sorry..."

"I'm sorry, too! Oh, let me apologize first. I never should have been so judgmental of your new crew."

"And I should never have been so spacey! It's like I got to college and immediately dropped you! I really didn't mean to be such an epic jackass."

There's a pause, then we both break out into laughter. It's a relief. I didn't even realize what a burden it's been these past few weeks, not being able to confide in my old friend. Not that Tara and the new crew aren't wonderful people, but there's something about the friends you make first.

"You know what this reminds me of? That scene in Clueless where Cher and Tai make up at Travis' skateboarding thing."

"Does that make me Cher?"

"If the satin shoes fit..."

"I'm surprised, Z-Money. That's a very preppy movie for you to enjoy. I thought the whole valley girl, SoCal thing was 'not your speed.'"

I wait for a second on the line, breath bated as I test this joke. I want to clear the air fully, though Zooey's never been awesome at laughing at herself.

"I actually wanted to tell you something serious," she says, suddenly breathing heavily. "But I don't know how. So I think maybe I'm just gonna blurt it out."

"Is everything okay?"

"No. Yes! I mean, I'm fine, but—I just heard a few weeks ago about what you went through last year at school. With Ruben."

Hearing his name, even after all this time, sends a nasty jolt through my spine. Which makes me even angrier—that he still has power over me.

"Do you not want to talk about this at all?"

No. No. Never, ever again. But Zooey's voice is so plaintive that I do what I always do, and give in to her.

"I'm trying really hard to put it behind me. But...I mean, what do you wanna know?"

"I guess I don't have any questions. I just wish you could have felt comfortable enough to tell me. What you were going through. And, like, why you left."

"But Zooey, you've gotta understand. It was so private. And it wasn't—it's not—about you." The words sound harsh even in my teacher voice, but I'm proud of owning them. I feel the way I did in the library, with He-Who-Must-Not-Be-Named. There's no greater feeling, I begin to think, than owning exactly what you mean to say exactly when you mean to say it.

"That's not how I meant it. Crap." Zooey takes a sip of something, on her end of the phone. I try to imagine the party she's at. It's probably full of art kids, in all their alterna-glory. The scattered good old girls and boys from town. I loved Savannah, but I have to admit: I never felt like I was home there. I don't miss it.

"What I mean to say is: I'm so proud of you. And amazed and shocked and sad that you went through all that, all alone." Her voice is cracking, which of course drags me down, too. The contents of my dorm room begin to blur. "I'm here now," Zooey blubbers, finally. "That's what I want to say. Even though we're far apart, I want you to always know that I'm here for you. Okay?"

"Okay."

"And I won't ever judge you. And we can always talk."

"Okay."

There's the sound of our co-mingled, strangled-sounding breath, and then this too gives way to laughter.

"Happy birthday, Avery. Love you, bitch."

"Bye, Tai. Love you, too."

We click off, and I'm suddenly exhausted. The good kind of exhausted, though. The kind where all your bones feel sleepy and satisfied.

Who needs guys, I muse to myself as I flop face-down on my twin bed. When you have great friends?

* * *

I hear it in my dream, first. Lyrics, clear as a bell, seeming to sail from the ground up:

Now that it's all coming clearer,

Know that I wanna be your mirror

I'm sorry we're not all as strong

But know you're right, and I was wrong—

You are moon and you are sky,

You're the waves on the beach in the evening tide

You were past and now you're present

Please-oh-please...

"SHUT THE FUCK UP!"

...be with me..

"I WILL CALL CAMPUS SECURITY ON YOU, FUCKING LLOYD DOBLER!"

...AVERY...

I think it's my name that finally does the trick.

When my eyes slide open and I'm snapped back to reality, the first thing I see is Tara, crouched by our courtyard-facing window. She's staring down at something I quickly reconcile with the content of my dreams, looking serene in a pool of moonlight. When she sees me sit up, she beams with a genuineness I'm not accustomed to seeing on my slightly-scary friend. She beckons me over. And though I begin to awaken, it's all a little hard to believe.

The yelling person is an angry looking frat guy, three windows down. His bare and very pale chest glints in the moonlight. Other lights snap on along our floor and below. Somewhere, I think I hear a coyote, baying its dissent. But then I look down.

Brendan has planted himself firmly below my dorm room, with a wireless amp and his electric guitar. It's hard to make out much else in the darkness, but I hear a wistful quality in his voice. When the song appears to end, he starts up again. It's impossible, but for a second it feels like we make eye contact. I find his eyes in the darkness, just the way he found mine in a big crowd that first night at the Ruby Room.

You recognize love when you've never seen it before. And it's like that mumbo-jumbo suddenly makes sense. Who did I find in the darkness? Brendan. Who did I want, and who was I waiting for? Brendan. The knowledge is so deep and pure that it feels like something's clicked into place. I hear his voice reach up to me once more, and then I scream his name like a giddy school girl, or Kate Winslet in Titanic: "Brendan! Wait!"

I briefly consider leaping out the window into his arms, before common sense—in the form of Tara—intervenes. "Take the elevator, Avery," she says. Her eyes seem to share my magic, though. We're both on this crazy plane.

My slippers slap against the tile of our floor, likely rousing whoever wasn't already roused by the serenade. As I wait for the elevator, heart pounding—fuck it, it's taking too long, I'll go for the stairs—a memory slips across my conscious. That morning we met on the playground. The twin brother's shaggy hair and his Red Hot Chili Peppers t-shirt. He'd made me laugh so hard with that stupid "if-your-hand-is-bigger-than-your-face" joke that I remember falling into the wood chips right then and there, rolling into their fold.

"So you're the product of a broken home, too, huh?" Brendan had asked me, as his brother pivoted in another direction, in search of a soccer ball.

"Yep. It blows."

"It can blow," he'd said, the little wise guy. Even then, with the hair in his eyes. "But you know what? I can already tell you're interesting. And even shitty things don't keep truly interesting people down."

Chapter Twenty-Two

* * *

When I reach him, panting, he sets down his guitar on the grass. And it's a little bit awkward. Face to face, I'm forced to remember the reason we parted ways. Or more specifically—the leggy, buxom brunette in his room. I want to communicate my ecstasy at realizing I'm in love at the same time that I express disdain for that wreck of an evening. How to be an empowered woman who's also crazy smitten? While I'm thinking of the coolest way to pull this off, my mouth blurts out:

"Who was she?"

Brendan steps toward me, bringing with him that fiery man-smell. Tobacco and whiskey and something sweet and musky, mingling with the jasmine and honeysuckle that grows around our dorm entrance. It takes all my will not to flop into his arms when he comes close enough to touch me. I have missed him, I realize, so fucking much.

"My ex-girlfriend."

"Ex?"

"Yes. It wasn't as clean a break as I would have liked. When you started dating my brother, I entertained the possibility of a reconciliation."

"That's an elaborate way to say you were horny."

"Hey!" Brendan says, his eyes briefly serious. "Do you have any idea how hard that was to watch? The anointed Chase Kelly, swooping in and getting exactly what we both wanted, yet again? I don't know that you have the whole moral high ground here."

I bow my head, briefly ashamed. So much for Tara's rigmarole about being a sex-positive woman of the world. Is there a distinct part of me that's been thriving on the drama of being caught between brothers? Haven't I been a little evil, too, jerking these two boys around?

"I'm really sorry," I say, directing my words to his chest for fear of what his eyes will tell me. "I didn't mean for any of this to happen, Brendan."

"I didn't, either. And I'm sorry I haven't called. For a second there it seemed like a sign that you walked in on me while I was trying to leave Jenn a second time. And even if my brother bugs me, I didn't exactly want to steal his girlfriend." He takes a step closer. "Well. Until you showed up tonight, that is."

"Oh?"

"Honestly, Avery? The second I found out you were coming to SDU, I broke it off with Jenn. Before I even saw you. And you know why?"

I just shake my head. Above us, the sleepless jock slams his windows shut, pleased with the halt in the noise.

"Are you really gonna make me say it?"

"You've been coy enough, Mr. Kelly. Let's have it all out on the table."

He smiles, with half of his perfect mouth. I drink in the pillars of his scooped shoulders. The grimy V-neck shirt, emblazoned with "The Velvet Underground" logo. The boy in front of me is not perfect, but he might just be perfect for me.

"Because I have never gotten over you, doofus. Not since we were little kids."

There's the sound of clapping above our heads, and with a giggle, I look up and see Tara. Beside her is the outline of RA Jeff, naked on top but for a fedora. Seems like love really is everywhere, tonight.

"It's you, Brendan!" I squeal, finally collapsing against him. "It's always been you. It just took me longer to see it."

We stumble into his bedroom, laughing. The guitar thunks against the edge of something hard, emitting a loud twang. Someone—Brendan's roommate, I gather—rises from the adjacent twin bed. With a loud grunt of displeasure, roomie grabs a pillow and heads out into the hallway. "Sorry, Paul!" Brendan breathes at his retreat, half-heartedly, but as soon as the door clicks shut and leaves us in cozy silence, we start to chortle again.

Then, Brendan takes my hand in his, beginning to run his fingers over my palm. He bends down to me, and our foreheads touch. I press my face upward, and am rewarded with a soft, sweet kiss that sends little electric shivers straight to my toes.

"Come to bed," he pleads, flicking a long blonde tendril away from his eyes. I nod, and allow myself to be led.

Brendan sits down on the mattress and spreads his legs—an invitation. I slide into the space he's made for me, and allow him to gather me in his strong arms. His shaggy head is level with my heaving breasts. He kisses the swell of my cleavage through the thin fabric of my night-shirt, and I can feel my nipples perking. I arch my back, to provide him a better vantage.

His hands rove around my back like caterpillars, and I find myself beginning to press against him rhythmically, sliding my hips back and forth against his taut pecs. Brendan tilts his head up and brings his hands to meet at the base of my neck, drawing me down. He kisses me deeply, with his eyes open. It's unsettling for a moment, but as his tongue presses past my teeth, beginning to make slow but assertive circles, I decide I like it. I like being so close to him, feeling so connected.

We kiss softly for a while longer, rearranging our heads this way and that so the moonlight sliding in from between the slats of gritty blinds catches us at fresh angles. Brendan digs his fingers into my back, beginning to massage my musculature. I sigh with pleasure at the touch.

"I want to taste you," he says, after whole days might have passed, and his voice is strong and serious, reminiscent of the way he sings. Before I can so much as nod my assent, Brendan eases me down to sitting beside him, and brings his own body to the floor with a heavy whump. He inches his knees towards me, arriving level at my hips. With one strong, flattened palm, he presses into my chest until I'm flush against his bedspread. Despite being the country of a twenty-one year old boy, his sheets and pillows are surprisingly soft. Some kind of jersey. I let the fabric embrace me.

Brendan nudges my own knocking knees aside with a jerk of his chin against my quivering thigh; his stubble grazes my sensitive flesh, causes me to spasm with a little premature delight. Then, he begins to kiss me. Softly and slowly, he plants a trail from the inside of one knee all the way up to the damp hollow of my pussy. With expert hands, he slides the paper-thin fabric of my pajama pants down from my ankles. The pants pool on the floor by my ankles, serving me up to the room.

Brendan begins to suck on me, teeth gently rubbing against the crook of my pubis. I widen my stance, feel myself begin to sink into this pleasure. It's a dizzying thing. I feel carried to the ceiling. He places his hands squarely on the tops of my thighs, beginning to knead me in concert with his kisses. This is the first time I cry out.

"Is it good, baby?" he murmurs into my skin, once again causing me to spasm with a tickle. I can only muster a laugh that's one part gasp. Sensing my encouragement, Brendan shifts his full lips by a few centimeters, and drags my soaked panties into his mouth. The sense of his tongue so close to my clit sends me up; I have to press my fingers hard against the sheets and bite my lower lip.

"I want you to scream, if it feels good," Brendan commands, intuiting my reserve. He plunges back into me, sucking at drenched cloth—and as his fingers still work my legs, his strong tongue finds purchase below the elastic. Our naked flesh touching does the trick once more, and this time, I do scream. I thrust my head backwards into the pillows, raising my hip bones to him so he can take more of me inside. In ready response, Brendan begins to lap at my puckered mound, driving his tongue back and forth in tiny circles. His fingers leave my thighs and rise to my panty-line. With more aggression than before, he rips my flimsy protection aside, easing me out of the shorts until I'm bare and utterly supine before him. I become aware of the room's chill on my naked pussy, but not for long. Brendan brings his fingers to my wet heat, and slowly pushes two inside my contracting center.

"Brendan," I cry to the ceiling. "Oh, fuck. Oh, God. Yes." When I glance down at his face, I see my lover's eyes screwed up with concentration and what I take to be delight. He continues to plumb me, work me, fingers now driving up against my G-spot as his tongue flicks back and forth at an improbably faster pace. Brendan brings his other hand up from its place on my thigh, and grabs my breast through my frail t-shirt. With minimal rooting, he finds my pert nipple and squeezes my tip lightly.

"I'm gonna come," I hear myself pant—though words and reason are long gone to sensation. I hear ringing in my ears again, as I had at the beach just yesterday. My brow-line is drenched with sweat. My sex is awake to Brendan's body in a way it's never been to anyone's before. My breasts feel swollen, my nipples are hard as rocks. I'm already aware of how slippery my nethers have become—and they're even wetter, somehow, than they were the other day at the beach. Or in any of my daydreams. Oh, fuck. Oh, fuck, I am going to come...

I tell Brendan as much, and right as I'm rising to orgasm like the crest of a wave, he withdraws, grinning. My body squirms at his vacancy. I writhe against the pillows, whimpering, wanting him bad.

"Wait," Brendan murmurs, neatly wiping his mouth of me. With deliberate motion, he brings his hands to his jeans, unbuttons himself slowly. I'm humping air, still dizzy with want. After much fanfare, he drops his pants and eases his erect manhood out for me. Once more I'm confronted with Brendan's perfect penis: he is straight and rigid as a post, pink perfection rising from a small thatch of golden hair. He grins at me in question, and I nod like a maniac. Then, Brendan mounts me. Brendan slides inside.

I sigh with pleasure as he eases toward my top, filling me in a way that makes me feel as if I were empty before. I sense myself curving around him, holding him fast—and when I look up, I see that his eyes are filled with emotion. We hover like this for a moment, before he regains composure and pulls nearly all the way out. But no sooner is he almost away from me than I crave him again.

Brendan pushes back and forth inside me, increasing his pace and rhythm. He begins to wrap his body around me, as if seeking to infuse our two vessels. He drags one hand up to my soaked hair, raking his fingers across my scalp. In response, I dig my nails onto his back. After a mere minute or two's thrusting, I find myself hovering at the tip again.

"I'm gonna come," I moan again, raising myself slightly so I can feel his thrusts against my G-spot. I groan. I reach a hand backward until I find the wall, where I press my sweaty palm against the cool concrete.

"Not yet!" Brendan laughs. He pulls out again, then very quickly flips me over, so I'm lying face-down. With some surprisingly welcome roughness, he raises my hips up toward his, indicating that he wants me on all fours.

I've never tried this position before. I feel my heart begin to rattle against the cage of my chest—half with desire, half with nerves.

But Brendan's entrance from behind is slow and cautious. He places one palm on the swell of my ass, then drives deep. I'm shocked at the new ceiling of pleasure we've discovered—to the extent that I cry out. I can feel more of him, he can sink deeper...in instinctual response, I push my rear against his cock, letting him know I want it this way. Brendan reaches back up to my hair and entwines his fingers in my damp blonde tresses, drawing me back towards him. He starts to ram me harder and faster.

"Yes," he says, through gritted teeth. Glancing over my shoulder, I'm afforded the pleasing view of his glistening naked chest. I don't remember when he took off his shirt, but I weaken even further at the sight of his engaged six pack, the muscles involved in penetrating me. His face is twisted up with something like hunger. There is the pushing, the grunts of effort, the wet slapping sound he makes against my skin...

"I'm gonna come, Avery," he says. I stumble for a moment at his use of my name in such a crucial moment. Glancing over my shoulder again, our eyes meet. My spine arches in tandem with his eyebrows, and suddenly I am filled with a hot liquid. Brendan collapses over me, breathing heavily, clammy hands fumbling for my swinging breasts. He stays inside of me, remaining erect. I feel nearly as relieved and sated by our union.

He breathes sweetly against my ear, kisses gently along the nape of my neck. The expanse of my skin feels soft and tender. Our flesh cools together. Moonlight stripes us.

"And now it's your turn," Brendan says darkly, laughing against the nape of my neck. His breath tickles me again, and my spine curves away from him. Reading this as invitation, Brendan presses into me again. I'm shocked he's still hard, but at the same time, I hear myself sigh with relief.

"Yes," I say, ordering him. "Fuck me. Fuck me until I come. Hard." Who is this woman, with her dirty-talk? I don't pause to consider, but rather reach a hand around to grip one of Brendan's taut buttocks. His breath comes faster at my aggression, and he picks up the pace again, driving harder and faster. He brings one hand from my breast down to my clit, and begins to rub me gently as he drives inside.

"Yes," I say, my voice taking on the qualities of a scream. "Yes!" He pushes and pushes, rams me hard. I swell as I had before, in his mouth. I recall us on the beach, sweaty and sandy and lusty, lacking abandon.

Our rhythm has become a blur of movement and sound. It sounds absurd, but there are seconds where I cannot say for sure where he ends and I begin. I feel the color rising in my face again, the delicious wash of feeling beginning in my belly. Brendan drags a hand down my back, up my front. He caresses my chest. He kisses my back. He pries his working fingers from my desperate clit and brings them to my mouth, where I draw them inside. I suck the taste of both of us from his prints, arch my head, and then come. I come with a shuddering flood and a great sound, drenching his cock. My thighs tense and release. And when it's finally, finally over, I fall flush against the mattress, giggling.

We don't talk for a moment. We just breathe. It's like we've just escaped enemy fire—there is a quality of relief in our panting. Slowly, Brendan rolls away from me, leaving me briefly cold. But the absence of skin doesn't last long; he tucks his legs against mine, drapes us both with a blanket, and makes a little spoon of me.

We fall asleep, tangled in one another. Just so.

Chapter Twenty-Three

* * *

The morning is marked by two uncomfortable, immediate realizations: 1) sometime in the night, Brendan's roommate has returned. I know this because he's snoring loudly, in the twin bed catty corner to us. 2) It's Monday, meaning a lecture from Her Highness Chen is imminent.

But no sooner have I registered the unpleasantries than I take a moment to bask in their opposites. Namely, Brendan's body—as perfect and lovely as it seemed to me the night before, still wrapped around mine. His chest rises and falls sweetly, as if puffing up with pride. His sleeping expression, obscured by the flop of golden hair, is near-angelic. I don't want to wake him up because his furrowed eyebrows and smiling mouth are so endearing. Instead, I turn to him and place an exploratory finger on the tip of his nose—for no other reason than to remind myself that this really happened. We really happened.

The rest of the previous night comes rushing in: my birthday tantrum, my talk with Zooey, my Say Anything-style serenade. There was a fairy-tale like gauze hanging over the previous evening. I wasn't entirely convinced it had all happened, and wasn't some elaborate dream.

"Good morning, sunshine," Brendan whispers, surprising me. His eyes remain screwed closed, but his mouth breaks into an easy smile.

"Are you for real, Mr. Kelly?"

"I'm always for real, Ms. Lynne."

Across the dorm, Brendan's roommate emits a particularly gross snore. I stretch my arms above my head and rise to sitting, releasing a yawn. In the light of day, I'm struck again by how clean Brendan's dorm is. But for the musical bric-a-brac, it's pretty tidy for a teenage boy.

"What are you thinking?" Brendan asks, finally opening his eyes. Even crusty with sleep, his gaze is all the assurance I need. His oceanic irises tell me: Yes, it was real. And so it remains. *

We stumble to class late, hand in hand. I'm wearing an extra-long band t-shirt (for a group called De La Soul), belted at the waist with one of Brendan's guitar straps. Having not fit into any of his shoes, I'm still wearing my bunny slippers from the night before—but it's not like I really care. My hair's a mess, too, but that's actually because yours truly has been engaging in morning sex. In the communal shower. 'Cuz you gotta honor the bucket list. Mmm.

Brendan smiles at me in a dopey way over his mirrored John Lennon sunglasses, looking cute as hell in a sleeveless black top, skinny jeans and one day's growth of stubble. We share a breakfast burrito, at his insistence. "These are the best in the city, and they're right on campus," he tells me, while waving away my money at the Podunk little stand. From the first bite on, it's heaven. It seems that even the San Diego food vendors association seems to be smiling on our union.

And I can't stop giggling. I'm not even phased when Professor Chen cuts her eyes at the pair of us, frowning at our joined hands. "Everyone please pull out the Forster essay," she says, peering hawkishly at our class. "And let's hear a quick distillation of this work. One or two sentences on the theme. Any takers?" She doesn't give the room so much as a moment to compose itself before riveting her eyes on me. "Avery Lynne," the lady says. "Can you summarize for us?"

I can feel Brendan stiffen beside me, in solidarity. The whole humming room seems to draw breath. And sure, I'm Angry Avery in this moment. I don't appreciate being pinned to lower expectations. I don't enjoy being made a fool of. And for once, given that I've spent the past week steadfastly avoiding the male gaze, I have an answer.

"Forster's treatise is self-explanatory and eponymous. As is the case in all of his novels, he's chiefly concerned with the human ability—and moral significance—of people striving to communicate successfully with one another. The essay is about humanity at the same time it's about a writer's obligation, as crystallized in the quote: 'Only connect the prose and passion, and both will be exalted.'"

A charged hush falls over the room as my classmates swivel back towards Professor Chen. Beside me, Brendan swallows. It's all ridiculously out of proportion, in my opinion. I mean, you can call me a lot of things, but stupid isn't one of them.

"That's fine," our teacher says finally, her lips curling into a smile. She nods once at me, eyes shifting only briefly to my seatmate. Brendan reaches over, below the table, and squeezes my thigh with appreciation. When I catch his eye, he's beaming at me, all pride and surprise. So this is what feels like, I think to myself, dizzy and chipper. To have someone fully in your corner. Because I could get used to this.

Though we pay far less attention throughout the remainder of the Forster lecture—Brendan keeps making eyes at me, and I keep doodling erotic cartoons in the margins of my notebook where he can see—I'm surprised at how quickly the time flies. Brendan buries his lips in my scalp as we rise and gather our things, before reaching down to pinch me lightly on the ass. I squeal with delight as our classmates shake their heads, repulsed. But I still don't care! Ha! No one can rain on my parade today. Absolutely no one.

We pause at the top of the Hampton Hall stairs, poised in a beam of sunlight. Brendan takes my face in his hands. "You look beautiful like this," he says, eyes flickering back and forth between my own pupils, as if they can't bear to rest on just one part of me. "A perfect muse."

"You're not so bad yourself, mister." I reach up and playfully tug on his lower lip with my front teeth, drawing him down toward me. We laugh together, syrupy and goofy and gross, and I'm just about to fold myself into the sweet cage of his arms when—

"What the fuck is all this?"

—a dark cloud descends. My heart plummets at the familiar voice.

"Chase, listen," Brendan is saying above my head, sounding meek in protest—but this is a battle I know I can't let him fight for me. We're both to blame for giving in to passion.

"You scamming on my girl, brother?"

"It's not like that, man. You know it's not."

"Don't fucking tell me what I know..."

"Chase, please. Listen. This is my fault. I should never have –"

"Shut up, bitch!" The atmosphere in the air seems to shift at the harsh word rendered. I turn to face Chase, plant my feet squarely. I search his eyes for any inkling of the compassion he's shown me previously, but I can't get through to him. Not least because he's wearing mirrored Aviator sunglasses that remind me of the Terminator.

"Don't you fucking call her that! Listen. Bro, we never meant to hurt you. Honest." They sound just like the little boys I knew, in one way. Brendan's tone is wry and slightly whiny, while Chase is authoritative and flat. But something darker lies beneath both.

"FIGHT, FIGHT, FIGHT!" some kid shouts from the bottom of the stairs, and it's then that I realize what I'm witnessing. From the lower vantage, it's clear that these two hulking, strong men are about to wail on one another. I step up, between them.

"Don't you bro me, Brendan. What? You think since you're all rock-star now, you get a piece of my ass?"

"She's not a piece of ass. She's been our friend since we were kids. And don't you even give me this shit, like you haven't always known how I felt about her."

At this, Chase merely smiles a warped, unrecognizable smile—one of possession, and cruelty. What happens next is fast: the elder Kelly coils his fist, reaches his arm behind his head like he's throwing a javelin, and then sinks a punch into his brother. Square in the jaw.

I scream, obscuring some of the sickening crunching noise that comes from Brendan's face. That's the thing about a punch—it doesn't sound quite how the movies would have you believe. I think for a moment that Brendan's jaw has been broken, but after a moment's staggering, he rights himself. I run up to his side, thinking I can create a barrier between the brothers—but Brendan firmly motions me aside.

"Avery, this is older than you," my lover says, jamming the blonde hair back behind his ears like it's the source of his fury. Then, Brendan grits his teeth. He cracks his knuckles—the picture of a cartoon villain. A small crowd of onlookers has begun to gather around the Hampton steps, each of them so fascinated by the prospect of a fight in our peaceful, "Hang 10" SoCal that they could be munching on popcorn.

"Guys, please," I try again, this time allowing a thickness to enter my voice. This is truly the last thing I wanted—the last thing I thought of, even, while deliberately not thinking about my situation with the Kelly brothers. But on seeing his brother's preparations to retaliate, Chase has turned his attention back to the fight. He bounces from foot to foot like a boxer, and begins taking swings at his brother again. This round, Brendan has the presence of mind to duck.

He's light on his feet—especially compared to Chase's slightly clumsy, rage-fueled motions. One boy appears all muscle, and the other all skill. I know it's neither the time nor place, but their divergent body types have never struck me so much. I think of Chase's heavy breathing on our runs, and mentally compare these to the muscular curve of Brendan's back as he flexed himself inside of me just last night. But now is surely not the time for a mental tally. I start screaming again: Stop, you guys! Don't be stupid!

Out of nowhere, Tara, Trevor and RA Jeff emerge and secure themselves around my elbows—and my friends seem as titillated by the street fight as the cooing crowd.

"Go Brendan!" RA Jeff hollers, pumping a fist in the air.

Trevor shoots him a look. "You mean, go Chase! Chase is the one who called Avery all those times. He's Mr. Perfect."

"Chase also just called our girl a bitch, and is not doing himself any favors with the Cro-Magnon act," Tara trumpets. She rubs me on the shoulders, as my eyes swing from brother to brother. So far, no more punches have landed—but Brendan's artful dodging is infuriating his brother. If they didn't seem hell-bent before, they sure are now. Chase tosses his glasses aside, and I see that the look in his eyes transcends something. Some human impulse has left his face. It's like watching a shark's eyes roll into kill mode. I am suddenly truly afraid.

"Boys! Chase! Stop it! We can talk about this!" Not quite having a plan, I take a step or two into the designated 'ring' around my fighting suitors. Brendan sees me do this, and his eyes tighten with shock.

"Baby, get out of the way!"

"No! I won't let you guys do this. It's stupid! You're brothers!" I take another two steps into the center, so I'm between Chase and Brendan.

"This is so rich. And you've been with Melora this whole time, Chase! I don't know what your deal is!"

These words—this revelation, rather— pinches something inside of me, but it does something worse to Chase. The older Kelly paces and snorts like a bull seeing red, and doesn't appear at all phased that a girl has entered his ring. Instead, without looking at me, he cocks his bruised fist back and roars before letting loose the second punch to find flesh.

He aims well over my shoulder, but his eyes are fixed on Brendan—to the extent that he doesn't notice I'm in slippers, standing on the precarious edge of a long stone staircase. When I see his fist coming, I know a terror I've only experienced once before. I'm horrified to see such cruelty in this face I know so well. It makes me duck, involuntarily. Which makes me slip. Which makes me fall.

I'm dimly aware that Brendan is cowering, clutching his left eye—but only dimly. Tumbling backward down the stairs, my stomach flips up and down. At first, I seek purchase. My hands and feet reach out for anything in my path—the legs of people, the stones themselves. But in another few seconds, I give in to the dull pain assaulting me from all sides. I feel stone on the side of my head, and stone against my shoulder, and stone against my stomach. Everything hurts. I know the staircase can't be this long. I hear screaming, but can't locate where it's coming from. Finally, I collapse in a heap, heart pounding, limbs aching—and my intelligent, battered body makes a choice: darkness.

Chapter Twenty-Four

* * *

When I wake up, I see: an icky, brown stain on an otherwise sterile-looking white ceiling. Light; excessive, aluminum light. One flickering panel of fluorescents guards a window, which is slightly open so I can hear and smell the outside. It only takes another second to confirm that I'm in San Diego, which I deduce because from the perfume of jasmine, and the baying of seagulls.

My eyes are sore, which is strange. They feel weary and wet. Still, I let them travel to a bedside table, where they discover three—no, four!—elaborate floral arrangements, each of them fixed in long plastic drinking glasses. The first is a suggestive red orchid. Beside this, there's a hearty mixed bouquet of white and red roses. In the largest glass, there's a bundle of what I take to be pseudo-flowers—long stems made of wire, crowned by mini-collages and buttons. And finally, there's an exuberant bunch of wild-flowers, knotted with red ribbon. These, I decide, are the true source of the jasmine smell.

Though the beauty by my bedside makes me smile, the next sensations I know are pain. A dull pain, induced by any kind of movement, threads most of my body. I open my mouth to find that my teeth feel fuzzy, and my lips are cracked. I immediately wonder how long it's been since I last showered—and accordingly, how much water could hurt me, given the current state of affairs.

"There she is," my father says, making himself known before I can even account for his location in the room. "There's my pretty girl!" He sounds tired. I swivel my neck and find Pa in a hospital chair, rubbing his eyes like he's just woken up from a nap. I'm not used to seeing my father so unkempt. He's got three days' worth of beard and his typically gelled hair is tousled. Fresh worry lines are etched in his face.

"Do you know where you are, sweetheart?" Frank says, bending towards me, taking my palm in his.

"I've got a wild guess."

"See your sense of humor is intact. That's aces."

We share a silent moment, the old man and me. I realize, on regarding his sweet brown eyes and dumpy suit, how much I've missed him. How much he's probably been missing me.

"You're going to be just fine," Dad says, sweeping my brow just as I'm beginning to articulate my sappy rejoinder. "And look at all these flowers, huh? Someone's got a big fan club." He rises and makes for the window. The light coming in through the blinds tells me that it's the end of the day. This prompts more realization. The passage of time, the presence of flowers, the sickening crunch of bone on bone...suddenly, memory intervenes, and I can think of only one man. Where is Brendan?

"Dad," I say, voice parched. "Brendan Kelly. Did you see him? Is he okay?" I try to sit up, but my back protests.

My Dad puts a finger to his chapped lips, and motions me back against the pillows. He tiptoes the length of my hospital room, then, with a magician's flourish, pulls aside the curtain separating my bed from what must be another patient's. There, coiled up in scratchy-looking regulation blankets and thin pillows, is my man.

The skin around his eye is blue, and shiny with some sort of cream. His hair is damp-looking, and falls sweetly against his face. His sleeping face bears the same concerned look as it did that morning, in his dorm room. This is the face of someone who cares deeply. As if in response, he groans in his sleep, and tosses a blanket aside.

"Avery, sweetheart! Don't cry!" My Dad rushes back to my bedside, ready to proffer water or a cool compress— but I have no real explanation for the water works. Only that something aches in me, to see Brendan sleeping like that. To see anyone loving me so very much.

"I'm okay," I bluster, all snotty and teary and pained. My father rubs my head. The world closes in again.

* * *

The next time I wake up, I believe it to be morning. The window light has a fresh quality, and the sounds outside indicate early commuters. I yawn and attempt a stretch, raising my sore arms above my head. I note that my biceps are covered with dark purple bruises, though some of the general pain seems to have subsided. I also feel less foggy than yesterday.

When I turn, ecstatic, to the bed beside me—I'm disappointed. It's empty, and made. Brendan has apparently gone. I turn as fast as my neck will let me towards the flowers on my night-stand, and am relieved to find my little trophies still there. Everybody looks a little un-watered, but it appears I didn't dream my visitors. People have cared about me. People have come. There's even a new bouquet, I discover, with a sleuth's delight. Yellow tulips, secured in a vase that's covered with

Edwardian script. I think I can faintly determine the words along the mouth of the glass: only connect...

I hear voices in the hall, then—three young-sounding people, conversing in the way of three young-sounding people who aren't trying super hard to be quiet. Two women and a man. One woman is saying to the other: "She's not ready for big groups yet," while the man is speaking over them both. In another heartbeat, the door to my hospital room has eked open, admitting two of the last people I'd ever hoped to see at my near-death bedside: Chase Fucking Kelly and Melora Fucking Handy.

They can tell they're unwanted. Chase shifts from foot to foot and doesn't look right into my eyes, while Melora—carrying a big ugly teddy bear, of the cheap variety one wins at fairs—immediately bites her lip and bugs out her eyes. I must look worse than I feel, I decide. Great. Let them know what utter dirt bags they are. Let them simmer in it.

"Hey, Avery," Chase starts, taking a gallant step towards me. I purse my lips. That's when I realize that the two of them are holding hands. Today, Melora is strawberry blonde, just about stitched into a pair of hip-hugging skinny jeans and a t-shirt that manages to be both low cut and midriff-baring. 'Midriff-baring.' Ugh, I sound like someone's grandmother. Is this what a violent tumble down a stone staircase will do to a sex-positive lass? Turn her into a prude?

"I don't even know where to start," Chase says. His voice catches, containing tears. I'm not quite ready to look at him, though. He's not going to earn my forgiveness so easily.

"I want you to know that I'm really deeply sorry," he continues, while daring to take one more step into my safe space. "I've never—I would never—it was honestly never my plan to hurt you."

"Yet you did."

"Yes. I did."

"And you hurt your brother, too."

Do my eyes deceive me, or is Chase Kelly cracking the ghost of a smile right now? I long for something to throw at his square, thug-like head. I wonder how I could have ever fallen for this act. All the while, he was just a brute.

"Should I go?" Melora asks, her glossy mouth screwed up, uncomfortable. Chase just shakes his head no, and seems to grip her fingers tight.

"I fight with my brother all the time. That doesn't really mean anything."

"So you're not sorry?!"

"No, no—I definitely am. But I've talked to Brendan. We can get through things like this. Our concern for the moment is you."

I'm secretly loving how awkward Melora is as she bears witness to this conversation. A pettier part of my mind is wondering: did she know about me and Chase? Was it at all true, what Brendan yelled on the steps about their ongoing affair? I figure then, if I'll ever have a moment to ask, this is probably it.

"Are you two really dating?" I blurt. The words tumble out so fast that I choke on them, and have to lunge for the water glass by my head. To my surprise, Melora swoops towards me and brings the cup to my lips, her movements as expert as a nurse's. I tilt my head back and sip slowly as she speaks, her tone professional:

"My family is actually ultra conservative, Avery. They've never wanted me to date, and they've certainly never wanted me to hitch up with a guy like Chase. So we've had a secret thing going for a while, but for a lot of complicated reasons nobody really can know about it. Drink."

I swallow the last of the water, curiosity piqued. I don't even take a moment to affect shyness at Melora

Handy seeing me battered in a hospital, like a body being taken apart for science. So he never liked me. I was an elaborate beard, all along. On some level, this news should be shocking—but it's either the effect of painkillers or the complexities of my own conscience that prevent me from being truly angry with Chase. I mean, about this particular wrongdoing, anyways.

"You were always such a good friend. I'm so sorry to have treated you poorly." The man of the hour continues to blubber in the doorway, looking fairly goofy with the big ugly bear between his fists.

"Wait, wait—so if our whole 'relationship' was a prop, why did you get so mad at me and Brendan?" Melora, who's been fluffing the pillows behind my greasy head this whole time, pauses in her ministrations for a second. I take it she's been wondering this as much as I have.

To my mixed glee and surprise, Chase just shrugs. His eyes are bleary. Considering his prop, he looks like nothing so much as a toddler who's been separated from his family in a grocery store. I can't help but laugh a bit, though the task hurts my ribs.

"I'm working on some anger issues," he says, furrowing his brow at my guffaws. "And Brendan and I—

we've always had this competitive thing going. He's this rock star musician, and he's smart, and all the girls like him..."

"I like you!" Melora cries.

"I liked you, too, come to think of it," I echo. "That is, until I discovered you were a possessive, lying, violent sack of shit."

"I deserve that."

"Absolutely you do."

"But think about it, Avery. You never really liked me. You liked this jock-y idea of me. And that's always how it's been, everywhere I go—people fall for this Homecoming King notion of Chase Kelly. You know I'm not even that good at football?"

"It's the hair."

"You laugh, but—I mean, I'm not witty. I'm not talented. What will I even have when college is over?" Melora, reading some cue, backs away from me. The two of them resume an eerily familiar American Gothic pose—him beside her, her beside him. It looks...right. Pathetic and a little sad, but right.

"I'm not quite ready to forgive you, Chase," I say finally, after a moment watching the couple-of-the-year coexist. My words seem to hurt him—he wrinkles up his face as if about to cry again—but Melora pats him swiftly on the back.

"Not yet," I amend. "Maybe soon, but...not yet."

"Sure," Chase musters. "But Avery? Can I ask you one favor? I realize I'm in no position to ask favors."

"I haven't decided yet if I'm going to press charges, actually."

"Jesus! Not that, it's just—look. My brother's really in love with you. I think you deserve each other. Just, be good to him, okay?"

I'm a little offended that he feels he has to ask, but Chase is making such a spectacle that I allow him one magnanimous nod. Some part of me knows that we're all young and resilient, and this is the time to be making mistakes. Maybe he'll change. Maybe I will.

"Yes," I say through a yawn, suddenly tired again. Suddenly lonely again. My body misses Brendan. "I'll be good to him." Epilogue: Six Months Later San Diego, 2014

"Wait! Mind the precious cargo!" In one daring leap, Brendan launches over the nubby, orange hand-me-down couch that an unenthusiastic duo of enlisted bandmates is currently hauling into our living room. His eyes are fixed

on a guitar without its case. A.K.A.: an extreme no-no in
our world.

"You said to grab everything from the station
wagon!" Tara whines, a half-smoked American Spirit
dangling languidly from the corner of her mouth. "I'm just
doing what I'm told, friend-o."

"My babies need their blankets," Brendan says,
taking the ragged red Fender from my friend's grasp and
carrying it into the house like a queen on a chaise. I laugh
at his affect, and he tosses his hair like a pony's mane in
response. The shaggy blonde is getting a bit out of control.
Brendan's hair now more-than grazes his shoulders.

(The shoulders themselves, I should say, have only
improved with time. Since we've both started taking ju-
jitsu—"In case my brother comes for us again, har dee
har"—the sinewy Kelly has added some considerable bulk.
Not that I care about such things, but for what it's worth.)

When he returns from the house, looking content,
Brendan takes a moment to regard our lawn. It's only a
tiny adobe number within walking distance of SDU, but
it's all ours. "I dub this love nest... loved!" my boyfriend
pronounces, then looks over at me. The grin he cracks is
the same one I've come to know well after all this time, but

boy does it still get me. That slight dimple in his tan face. That crinkle of stubble. The glinting white teeth.

"Get up here, Mrs!"

"Mrs? Did I miss something?" This voice is Trevor's. He has been the least helpful of our "help you move in" friends, having taken up camp pretty early on this morning in our house's best feature: the hammock strung between two palms in the front yard.

"Oh, he wishes," I coo, in my best Southern Belle. I run to Brendan like we're in Born Free, relishing the moment I reach him and collapse giggling into his arms. He pivots me neatly by the hips, then begins to kiss my face. He begins at the crown of my forehead and continues the trail all the way to my chin. He kisses my eyelids. He kisses my earlobes. He kisses my neck, which is now bereft of my choppy blonde hair since this summer's pixie cut. That's right, world: I'm dating a guy with hair longer than mine. Welcome to SoCal.

Nic and Drummer (I keep forgetting his name) emerge from the front door couch-less, arms swinging. The red eyesore is apparently placed, and so they are apparently finished for the day. Tara struggles to carry the last object from RA Jeff's borrowed Bimmer into the foyer: a human-sized canvas portrait of the love of my life, centered around the deep, thrilling green of his eyes.

"Be careful with that one, too!" I holler—but Tara just shoots me a glare. We owe her (and Trev and Jeff) big time for the help today, though I've no doubt the favor will be repaid soon enough. So long as there are hot clubs opening up in San Diego, so long as Fuhgettaboutit lurks on the horizon—I will have favors to lend to Tara.

"Don't forget about the Whiskey-a-Go Go!" Brendan hollers, as our friends make their final retreat. His band-mates holler, echoing the good news. And they have every right to be giddy assholes—a tiny but tasteful record producer has showed some interest in the band's breakout EP (Runaway, since you asked), and as a result they've been booked at some pretty hot places up and down the coast. But nothing too far away, yet. The guitarist has grown roots, after all.

Together, we survey our new kingdom: four walls, a door, art and instruments galore. Jasmine in a vase on the mantel-piece. Preserved cards and well-wishes from our friends, family, Professor Chen. Even the big ugly bear from Melora and Chase has found a home—as a beanbag chair, in our den.

With a soft incline of his head, Brendan indicates I lead the way inside. The screen door flutters behind us. I'm dizzy with the feeling of home, and even dizzier when he puts his rough hands on my waist.

"Hello, lover," he whispers into the crook of my neck, and I'm aware that for the first time in our entire courtship, we rightfully and entirely have the place to ourselves. I press my ass against the bulge in his jeans. He slips his fingers just below my pants, beginning to knead the soft flesh of my hips. He begins cautiously, as usual—now more than ever, since I have three pins in my left leg.

Brendan begins to kiss along the back of my neck, tasting my salt from our day of moving. When he reaches the space where my shoulder blades join, he brings his palms around my body, coming to cup my heavy breasts. He massages my tits gently through my t-shirt, before shifting his attention down. He sinks, slowly, to his knees. His fingers find the bottom of my shirt and begin to snake up and under my nakedness, rediscovering my unbound breasts. (The scar on the side of my rib-cage has prevented me from comfortably wearing a bra for quite some time.)

His lips, shrouded in stubble, find and dwell on a spot just above my hips—but ever insatiable, Brendan's kisses begin to probe further down. He moves his hands to my pants, unbuttoning with quick, deft strokes. His hands no longer shake with me. When the fabric binding my legs falls to a heap about my ankles, Brendan begins to kiss along my thighs. He kisses the places where the pins are, where the damage has been done and forgotten, absolving every trace of my wounds.

"That's good," I coo, encouraging—as if he needs any. Brendan's fingers slide down the band of my panties, coming to rest on my pubis. He probes me gently, until he lands light and quick on my clit. As usual, the man knows how to push exactly the right buttons—which is, of course, a key factor in true love, at least according to The Englightened Orgasm. I feel my knees weaken against his chest as he begins to rub me, making me wet.

He starts to nibble at the surface of my ass, just as my jaw drops and I glance up to the ceiling that we now share. It is elegant white, painted over tin. I reach a hand behind myself and flutter my fingers across the damp expanse of his downy hair. Brendan gently pushes me forward, scooting his fingers up against my center. His mouth moves downward, toward the neat button of my ass. As he presses one digit inside of me, he begins to lap. I too grow hungry.

"Baby, won't you take me on the couch?" I ask, after a few moments of approaching ecstasy. Brendan rises somewhat reluctantly, and helps me step out of my jeans. I drag his Jimi Hendrix t-shirt off as he walks, revealing the muscled expanse of his back, bringing my hands to pray at the altars of his pecs and abs. I rove across his torso, loving the feel of him below my fingers. I stand on tiptoe and incline myself upward, so I can kiss his sweaty neck.

In one quick twist, Brendan lurches around and sweeps me up into his arms. It's such a surprise that I break out laughing, throwing my head back like a bride. He begins to kiss my breasts again, and I sit up in his arms so as to wiggle out of the t-shirt.

"Alright, Prince Charming!" I snort. "Take me to my chambers! And have your way with me!"

"You're ridiculous, Avery" Brendan replies, flopping me down on our couch and coming to frame my supine form. I find myself in his perfect eye. I know us both. "But that's why I love you so."

* * *

THE END

Also From Celia Loren:

The Vegas Titans Series

Devil's Kiss (Widowmakers Motorcycle Club) by Celia Loren

Crushing Beauty (Harbingers of Sorrow MC) by Celia Loren

Breaking Beauty (Devils Aces MC) by Celia Loren

Wrecking Beauty (Devils Reapers MC) by Celia Loren

Destroying Beauty (Hell Hounds MC) by Celia Loren

Betraying Beauty (Sons of Lucifer MC) by Celia Loren

The Satan's Sons Series

Satan's Property (Satan's Sons MC) by Celia Loren

Satan's Revenge (Satan's Sons MC) by Celia Loren

Printed in Great Britain
by Amazon.co.uk, Ltd.,
Marston Gate.